THERA AWAKENING®

a novella for Interplay's Stonekeep™
by Steve Jackson and David Pulver

THERA AWAKENING™

Layout and Design by Dave Gaines
Edited by Scott Everts
Illustrations by Spencer Kipe
Based on background material by Chris Taylor

An Interplay Book
Published by Interplay Productions
17922 Fitch Ave.
Interplay, CA 92714

Thera Awakening and Stonekeep are trademarks of Interplay Productions.

First Edition: October 1995

Printed in the United States of America

0 9 8 7 6 5 4 3 2 1

Chapter One

⋅⋆⋅

"Curse this weather!" the woman said. "It looks to rain till the gods return."

She was kneeling on a narrow, muddy track, raindrops spattering off her broad-brimmed hat. On either side of the trail stood huge oak and birch trees and tangled undergrowth. There was a faint sound of crickets. She brushed wet brown hair aside, stood up, and turned to face her companion. He was a young man, of average height but with broad shoulders and a stubble of beard, black like his hair. Like her, he wore a sword and dagger, light armor, a shield strapped on his back, and a hat to keep off the rain. Under it his green eyes glinted, catlike in the forest gloom.

"No tracks, Tam?" he said. Watch-Master Hoth had split the patrol into pairs to cover more ground, and they had been searching along the forest trail for nearly an hour. It was mid-afternoon. They would soon have to rejoin the other searchers if they were to return to the fort by dark.

"Nothing. If they came this far, the rain's covered it," the woman called Tam replied. She shook her head. "An entire trading caravan. A dozen armed men. There's no sign of them, Rathe. It's like the forest swallowed them up."

Rathe nodded thoughtfully. When the Seth party failed to return from their trading expedition, a patrol had been dispatched from Stonekeep to look for them. They'd found a two-day old track — and then lost it when a heavy rainfall turned the forest trails to mud. "Maybe the others have found something," he said.

"You think it was raiders?" Tam asked.

"Could be." Raiders — savage humans or the wild goblin-like throgs — sometimes attacked Stonekeep's logging or trading expeditions. That was what Watch-Master Hoth had believed, Rathe knew. But ... "It doesn't make sense, Tam. We've had good relations with the tribes of Khera Vale for over a year. That's why Master Seth sent out the trading caravan. And you remember what happened the last time throgs attacked an armed expedition."

"They got a bloody nose." Tam grinned wolfishly. The fierceness of the stone-age throg warriors was little match for the dwarf-wrought armor and iron swords of Stonekeep's warriors. Especially since the throgs could never stop fighting among themselves long enough to unite against humanity. "But maybe it wasn't raiders, Rathe. Maybe..."

Suddenly, Tam stopped, drawing her sword. A shadow was moving by a tree. Her sword whispered from her scabbard, but Rathe put a restraining hand on her arm.

"Wait," said Rathe. "It's Orvig. I'd recognize that shuffle anywhere."

"Aye, it's Orvig, ye blind loon," said a gruff voice. A small man— a dwarf — stepped out of the bushes. He nodded to Tam. "Fast on the draw, m'lass, but can't you tell a dwarf from a throg?" He took off his hat, shook it. Water sprayed out, and Tam cursed. He grimaced, then nodded to Rathe. "Your Watch-Master sent me over, m'boy. Hoth says get back down the track. He wants us to reach Fort Thunder before nightfall."

Tam perked up. She was already soaked to the skin. Getting to Fort Thunder sounded good to her.

"No one else found anything?" Rathe asked.

"He thinks its hopeless." The dwarf kicked a stone into a puddle.

"I fear he's right. Night's falling, and we'll find nothing in this weather. I just hope tomorrow..." He looked at Rathe, frowned when he saw the youth wasn't listening to him. "What is it?"

"The Seth party. Four pack mules. And no signs of raiders. And yet, they vanished off the trail. Perhaps they fled from something..." Rathe scratched the stubble of beard on his chin. "If I wanted to get away from someone," he said slowly "I'd head for high ground." He looked around, then spotted a low hill, half masked by a stand of juniper trees. "There, perhaps. I think we should check it out first."

Tam followed his gaze. The hill was some three hundred paces distant, almost invisible in the rain. It was pouring down steadily, ending any chance of picking up the trail they had lost.

"Aye," said the dwarf. "Any chance is better than none." Together, he and Rathe started off east, toward the hill.

"And no chance at all, more like," Tam said softly. Rathe was disobeying orders by not returning, but she knew better then to question him. The dwarf-woman who had accompanied Seth was Orvig's own clan-sister. Rathe and Orvig were close — Tam knew vaguely that he was a friend of Rathe's family. And Rathe was her superior officer. Sighing, her thoughts of a warm campfire and dry clothes banished, she shouldered her pack and followed them.

They moved up the hill in single file, scrambling through the brush. Rathe took the lead, with the dwarf following and Tam bringing up the rear. Despite his short legs, Orvig made good time up the hill, ducking under soggy branches that Tam had to push aside. She was silently cursing Rathe when he halted suddenly. Taken by surprise, Tam almost tripped over the dwarf.

Rathe struggled to find his voice. "It's the Seth party. They're... dead."

Orvig took one look. Then he groaned, turned away and covered his face with his cloak.

The hilltop was an abattoir. The wind was blowing east, or they would have smelled it. At least a dozen men and animals had died there.

Rathe had never seen such slaughter, and he felt his gorge rising, but he knew it must be far worse for Orvig, whose sister might be among the bodies.

A young man lay dead, ripped almost in half. A severed leg lay across his chest. Another sprawled corpse was mutilated beyond recognition. Rathe guessed there were a dozen bodies — the entire Seth party. Pack mules lay in the mud, slaughtered alongside their masters. That he had guessed so well, only to find this carnage, seemed to Rathe a cosmic joke. This was butchery, not battle. His fists clenched, and he felt a tide of anger swell within him. What had done this? Why?

"I don't think it was throgs or savages," Tam said. She gestured at one body, great chunks torn from it. "Something was... feeding. It must have been wild beasts. Mutants."

Rathe nodded agreement. Nothing remotely human killed this way, but the forests held many horrors beyond man's ken. Mutant animals. That was why all Stonekeep's logging and trading parties were armed. But it had been many seasons since an entire trading party had been lost.

Orvig shuffled over. He moved slowly, like an old man. His face was pale and drawn. "Have you found Jhen's body?" he asked.

"Not yet." Rathe said. He had seen no dwarf-sized corpses, but some of the bodies were torn to bits. He hated to think what Orvig would be going through. "Maybe she got away," he said, knowing it wasn't much.

"Dwarf-girl's a small morsel," said Tam. "Like as not, they carried her off as a snack."

Orvig jerked back. Rathe could have hit her. Instead, he put his arm around the dwarf's shoulder and simply glared. Tam looked down, abashed. "Count the bodies," he ordered her. He looked at the sky. It was getting darker. "Then we'll report back."

Orvig and Rathe walked slowly among the dead, seeking answers. Beside him was the body of a middle-aged man, the clothes now bloodstained rags, the head attached only by a thin strip of gristle. Rathe recognized the patrician features and sharp nose of Master Trader Seth, the leader of the doomed caravan.

Rathe shook his head sadly, then knelt down and closed the staring eyes. Seth had not been a friend or relative, but everyone in

Stonekeep knew everyone else, at least by reputation. This had been a decent, hard-working man, who had long since earned the right to stay home in safety. Seth had gone back into danger, over and over, because he was a good trader and the city needed him. Rathe hoped his death had been quick.

The Master Trader lay next to one of his pack mules. A dozen gaping wounds marred its body. Saddlebags hung loosely from a broken strap...

"Empty?" said Rathe slowly. He lifted the saddlebag, passed it over to Orvig.

Even in his grief, the dwarf's mind was sharp.

"It's empty?" His eyes widened. "Not beasts, then."

"Unless this one held food. Let's check the other bags before it gets too dark."

The story was the same. Packs and saddlebags were empty — and two were missing. Rathe called Tam over, from where she had been counting the bodies.

"Eleven dead," Tam reported. Rathe thought she looked a little green. "Including Master Seth and his deputy Lara." She glanced sideways at Orvig. "I haven't found your sister yet, but..."

"Never mind that," said Orvig harshly. "Rathe, tell her."

Rathe explained what they had found. "Did you see any tracks?" he asked.

"No," Tam said. "It's odd. Whatever killed them... oh."

"What?"

"No weapons. None of the dead have any weapons on them. Someone must have —" She paused, stared at Rathe. "That's crazy. Animals don't loot! It doesn't make sense."

Rathe looked westward. The sun was just beginning to fall below the horizon, but they had perhaps another hour of light. He was suddenly overcome with a feeling of being watched. They should leave here, he thought.

"It's time to report back," he said.

Watch-Master Hoth commanded ten troopers: seven men and three women. Orvig was along as an observer, since Stonekeep's

Dwarven community had a stake in the missing trade expedition. Hoth was a large man with equally large passions. When Rathe had arrived almost an hour late, he had worked himself up into a tearing rage. Rathe's news didn't alleviate the anger. Neither did being led to the site of the massacre. It merely deflected it.

"Savages," said Hoth. "It must have been savages. Or throgs." He spat on the ground. The Watch-Master rounded on Rathe, expression fierce. "You say you found the bodies almost an hour ago. Why didn't you report back immediately?"

Rathe was Watch-Second, Hoth's deputy leader, but this was only his first patrol since his promotion. Rathe felt that his actual reasons — a need to try to make sense of the slaughter — would be too hard to explain. But he had a good excuse. "I had to check for survivors," said Rathe. "Sir."

"And you found none, correct?"

"We counted the dead. Master Trader Seth and all of the caravan were among them. So were the pack animals. Jhen Stonemelter, the dwarf representative, was not. She might have escaped, or..."

"Or you might not have performed a thorough search."

"Yes, sir," Rathe answered stiffly. He clenched his teeth but kept his face stony. It didn't seem to matter to Hoth that he'd been berating him just a moment before for spending too much time with the bodies. At least the rain had stopped, for the moment. But now flies were buzzing around the corpses.

Hoth looked over to the hilltop, where Tam and the other soldiers were sorting through the bodies. They'd decided to bury them here. "Well, if the dwarf woman's here, we'll find her."

Out of the corner of his eye, Rathe saw Orvig. The dwarf was leaning against a tree, shaking his head. So far, there had been no sign of Jhen. Rathe could guess what his friend was going through. Dwarf family ties were very close.

"Sir, what could have killed them?" he asked Hoth.

"Savages, as I said." Hoth stared at the corpses being piled up. "They ambushed Seth and murdered his men, then hacked up the bodies to make it look like mutant animals did it. But they gave themselves away. Look at that mule there... and there. Those are sword wounds, plain and simple. And they topped it by stealing the trade goods."

"The caravan wasn't carrying anything especially valuable?"

"Not to us. Six bolts of cloth and three sealed casks of wine. A cask of iron nails. Simple goods, just to trade for herbs and hides." Hoth laughed, bitterly. "Why trade when you can steal, eh?"

"But why would they take the trouble to make it look like a beast attack, mutilate the bodies, even gather up any spent arrows — and then go ahead and steal the caravan's weapons and goods?"

But Hoth was shaking his head. "You give them too much credit. The average savage — or even throg — isn't that bright."

Rathe knew better, and he knew that Hoth knew better, too. With their primitive weapons, the savages had to be doubly stealthy and clever. But he couldn't contradict Hoth directly. Maybe if he changed the subject a bit... "I think we shouldn't pull out yet, sir. We could check out the savage village that Seth's party was attempting to reach. We can scout..."

"The trouble with you, Rathe, is that you think too much." Seeing the young soldier stiffen, Hoth softened his voice, patted Rathe on the shoulder. "Finding the bodies was good work, son, but let's not get carried away. One savage village wouldn't have the guts to attack one of our trading parties. It would have to be several. And if there are savages on the warpath, ten men won't be enough. The Council will want to put together a retaliatory expedition."

Rathe wasn't sure that was a good idea. They weren't even sure it had been savages. He decided to give it one more try.

"Sir, I don't..."

Hoth cut him off. "Don't worry, Watch-Second." His eyes glinted fiercely. "I'll make sure you have a position in it." He glanced at the sun. It was would be night soon. "But it's a full day's journey back to Fort Thunder and another two days to Stonekeep. I'd like to get moving before full dark. We'll camp a few miles from this cursed place."

Rathe sighed. "Yes, sir." The soldiers had finished burying the bodies. It had taken nearly two hours. Stonekeep's dead would rest in shallow graves on the hillside.

"Listen up," Hoth said. Heads turned to face him, the tired men and women leaning on camp shovels. When he was sure he had their attention, Hoth drew his sword. It gleamed dully in the light of the setting sun. "Seth came to trade with the savages. They massacred his people, then tried to cover it up. They failed. We have ten troopers. We can't pay them back. But we'll be back in force — and we'll punish the animals who did this if we have to burn every wildman village in Khera Vale to do it."

None of the men cheered, but many nodded grimly, Tam among them. Stonekeep's vengeance would be swift and merciless. Rathe just hoped it would be well-aimed.

Rathe noticed Orvig standing silently. He was staring away from the graves, toward the setting sun. Hoth's talk of vengeance would be cold comfort to him. Rathe almost wished they had found Jhen's body. Then Orvig could have laid her to rest. Or did he prefer faint hope to a bitter certainty? Maybe so.

He walked over to the dwarf, leaned down to put his arms around Orvig's shoulder. Orvig turned to face him.

"We still haven't found a body, Orvig," Rathe said gently. "Don't give up." He tried to sound hopeful. "Jhen's probably still alive. If the savages captured her..." Why should they, Rathe thought, if they killed everyone else? He struggled for something that made sense. "They know Dwarves are wealthy. Maybe they want a ransom. We can get her back."

"Huh," Orvig grunted. "Save it for the soldiers, boy." He fixed Rathe with his gaze, eyes dark. "I overheard your conversation with Hoth. I'm afraid your Tam had the right of it." He looked over at the fresh graves. The patrol was breaking camp. "Whatever ate them..." His voice broke. "Jhen's dead," he said simply, then lapsed into silence.

Rathe placed his hand on the dwarf's shoulder. They stood silently for a few moments. Then Orvig started to speak. "Jhen was nearly forty. My youngest sister." He sighed. "I remember when she first saw the sun. She was sixteen years old. It was a revelation to her."

Since the Devastation — the great magical disaster that had

nearly ended civilization — men and Dwarves had lived together, as partners. But they also lived apart. While humans dwelt in the upper levels of the great keeps, the Dwarves delved far below. The Dwarves were crafters and farmers, partners of mankind, growing the succulent mushrooms and forging the hard steel that Stonekeep needed, in exchange for the lumber and fresh food harvested by men. But they rarely ventured out into the light.

Orvig was still talking. "When I first came topside, I was frightened." He gestured. "Everything was so — open." He waved his hand.

Rathe nodded in understanding. He remembered his first time in the dwarf caverns under Stonekeep, visiting Orvig's cousin. The deep winding tunnels and the weight of stone pressing down had been almost too much for a seven-year-old boy.

"I was frightened, boy. But not Jhen. She loved it. Wind, light, animals..." He smiled. "Our parents despaired of her. She didn't want to be a stonemason or a chemist. She wanted to be a trader, to travel, see the world." Orvig sighed. He sounded old and sad. "The years pass by quickly. Time melts lives, boy."

They marched in single file down the narrow dirt road, eyes scanning the forest on either side, alert for any attacks from the savages — or whatever — that had annihilated Seth's party. Rathe, as Watch-Second, was in charge of the rear guard: Tam and two other troopers, Loric and Calvert. Orvig clumped along beside them.

Rathe noticed Loric seemed to be falling behind. He slowed his pace slightly until he was walking beside the soldier, a quiet, dour youth in his late teens, with a bushy red beard. Rathe glanced meaningfully into the forest.

"Seems quiet, doesn't it?" Rathe said. He kept his voice low.

"Yes, sir," Loric replied. His voice sounded a bit hoarse. "Do you think the savages did it?" A cough punctuated the end of his sentence.

"Probably," Rathe said. He figured the soldiers would be better off believing in savages then in nameless monsters. Nothing breeds fear like the unknown. "Sore throat, Loric?"

"It's nothing." He coughed again, reflexively. "I'll be all right, sir."

Rathe wasn't so sure, but telling Loric that would do nothing for him. Instead he smiled and patted the man on the shoulder. "We're making camp soon," he told him. Loric nodded.

"Loric's got a cold?" said a voice behind Rathe. It was Tam. She'd been looking more serious of late.

"He's got something," Rathe answered. He considered. "I'll give him a rest tonight. Digging graves didn't help." He noticed Orvig, lowered his voice.

Tam followed his glance. "I'm sorry, Rathe," she said quietly. Rathe guessed she was apologizing for her remark at the clearing. "I know you and the dwarf are close."

"I never knew my parents," Rathe replied. "They died when I was a baby. Orvig raised me."

"I'm sorry," Tam said. She was the youngest of seven children. She tried to imagine what it would be like to have no living kin, then gave up and changed the subject. "Have you ever seen a savage, Rathe?" asked Tam.

"Once before," Rathe told her. "I was on garrison duty at Fort Tara, during logging season, when two came to the fort to barter hides and fresh-killed meat."

"What were they like?" Tam asked.

"They were dressed in skins, and I remember they carried spears with flint tips." He shrugged. "I didn't get to talk to them — I was on kitchen duty that night."

Tam grinned, probably at the thought of an officer doing scut work. "That was before you became Watch-Second?"

Rathe nodded. "Right. But now I am." He grinned back at her. "So pick up your heels, soldier," he said. "Camp's a few miles off."

They marched for an hour before it was too dark to continue, then pitched camp a few hundred paces from the dirt road, on a grassy knoll beside a stream. Most of the soldiers dropped immediately — it had been a tiring day. Hoth set them to digging a latrine. They lacked the manpower to build a stockade, so two men would be on sentry duty at all times. Hoth wanted no campfire; after they dug the latrine, they ate cold trail rations. Tam and the other soldiers grumbled, but they saw the sense of it.

Loric's cough was no better. Ignoring the soldier's half-hearted protests, Rathe relieved him of watch duties and ordered him to get a full night's sleep. They'd split the extra watch time. Rathe had assigned himself the last watch, the hours before dawn. He made sure the rest of the troopers were bedded down, checked the sentries — Tam had first duty — and then unrolled his camp blanket. He spread it on the wet ground, pulled off his boots, and made himself a pillow with his pack, hands behind his head. With everything that had happened, he might not be able to sleep, but it was good to just stretch his legs...

Someone was shaking him and whispering his name. He opened his eyes. A dark shape squatted down next to him. It was Tam.

"Your watch," Tam murmured. She yawned tiredly. He stifled a yawn of his own and blinked sleep from his eyes. It was raining again, a light drizzle. "Any problems?" he asked sleepily. His back had a crick in it — probably a rock. His throat felt dry.

"No sign of anything," Tam said. She yawned again. "The night's quiet."

Rathe checked his pack. "Where's my canteen?"

Tam already had her boots off. She poked Rathe's warm bedding with her toe. "If I tell you, can I use your blanket?"

Rathe gave her his best glare. Tam relented, and reached under his blanket, produced the canteen. "You were sleeping on it," she said dryly. She lay down, yawned again. "Wake me when we're in Stonekeep. Sir." She pulled Rathe's blanket over her head.

Rathe stationed himself by a boulder and settled down for a long watch. He was responsible for the southern half of the camp; another soldier, Dren, had the north side. A full moon peeked out from behind the thick clouds. Rathe took care not to silhouette himself against it. He wasn't sure he knew what had killed the trading party, but he didn't want to find out from an arrow in the dark.

Something stirred. Rathe cocked his ear, listening. What was that noise? The rain had stopped some time ago, and the night air was still and wet, but dawn was an hour or more away. His eyes roved over the camp. The sleeping soldiers and Orvig were dark humps on the ground. He could barely make Dren out — that shape by the big tree, he thought. Now the only sounds were the faint snoring of one of the men — Loric, most likely — and the chirp of crickets and night birds. And there it was again. A faint slithering, very close. A snake? It didn't sound like a person.

Was the sound coming from the bushes, behind that tree? He swallowed hard, drew his sword, and advanced. A twig snapped, and something moved. He brushed a tree branch aside...

It was a woman. She was kneeling, semi-crouched, as if unsure whether to run or confront him. She looked about his age. She wore a short garment made of animal skins. Her wrists and ankles were encircled with copper bracelets. She raised a finger to her lips, smiled slightly, and shook her head. "Shush."

Rathe knew he should sound the alarm. Was it a trick to draw away the sentry? He looked carefully about, ready to yell if he saw any sign of a savage horde. The girl was obviously a savage, but she didn't seem hostile — and, Rathe admitted to himself, she was strangely attractive. She had tangled, dark hair, sharp features, and large eyes, green as his own. Her skin was smooth but deeply tanned, long limbs left bare by the short garment she wore. Rathe noticed a scar running down one cheek and scratches on her arms from branches and thorns, but it enhanced rather than diminished her appeal, giving her an air of coltish beauty. A wild wood spirit, come to life.

The girl tossed her hair away from her face and rose slowly, palms outstretched. "Greetings, Rathe," she said. Her voice was strangely accented but understandable.

"You know my name?" he whispered back, stunned.

Instead of answering immediately, the girl squatted down next to him. She looked him over, as if studying him — or the armor and weapons he wore. Then, as if liking what she saw, she nodded. "Aye — I saw you on the hill of the dead, by the slaughter-ground. The dwarf who lost a sister spoke your name."

"The hill of the dead?" So someone had been watching! "Why did you come there?"

"I don't know." She cocked her head sideways. "There's something about you ... I came to warn you."

"Who slew them? Was it your people?"

"My folk?" She tossed her hair angrily, stood up in one fluid motion. "You dare — " Her eyes glittered. "The foe is the Tse'Mara, boy. The whispering death is coming on bloodstained wings. They'll be here before dawn. Get your men ready."

"The Tse'Mara —" The name meant nothing to Rathe. He also didn't like being called "boy" by someone who looked younger than him. "Who are you?"

"I'm Kel," she said impatiently. "The Tse'Mara — " She stopped suddenly, then listened. "Someone's coming."

Rathe glanced over his shoulder. It was Dren. When he looked back she was gone. He heard branches swishing. He could chase her, or...

"Rathe," Dren said. He was a grizzled veteran of maybe thirty-three years. "I thought I heard voices." He took in Rathe's drawn sword, and his eyes widened.

"You did," Rathe said. "Wake the Watch-Master. Now!"

The camp was soon roused, the men buckling on armor and readying swords. Rathe didn't think Hoth believed the girl's story — in fact, Rathe thought, he wasn't sure Hoth believed him at all.

"But where there's one savage, there may be more. And that means we stand to arms," Hoth had concluded.

"If they're hostile, why alert us?" Rathe asked. "I think she was telling the truth."

"Do you?" Hoth stood up. "Where's my sword?"

Dren handed it to him.

"This whispering death?" Hoth buckled on the sword, then used his helmet to splash water on his face. He coughed. "She claimed they attacked the caravan?"

"Yes," Rathe replied. "And were on their way here... on blood-stained wings."

"Huh. Birds?" said Hoth doubtfully. He rubbed the helmet with his cloak, drying it. "A trick of some sort?"

But Rathe wasn't listening. He was looking up. A faint humming noise was coming from high amid the trees.

And the Whispering Death swarmed down from the sky.

Hoth died without even a scream. Rathe only had time for a

quick impression — black body, glittering armor, a flurry of wings — and then Hoth was on the ground, the thing on his back, snapping at his neck with huge glittering jaws. A splash of blood, and Hoth's head rolled on the ground.

The soldiers flailed at them, swords slashing in the air. Another of the things swept down. Rathe saw spikes lash out. A man — Rathe thought it was Warren — went down, clutching at an eye socket. One of them flew at Rathe. He dodged and it passed overhead. A woman behind him was slower — Rathe heard her death scream. The thing buzzed overhead, blood spattering down.

Whispering death.

"Form a circle!" Rathe shouted. "Pull together. Raise your shields!"

Rathe's voice steadied them. The soldiers clumped together, forming an iron tortoise. Orvig was with them, his short sword out. Not everyone had a shield — Tam, Orvig and another trooper hadn't had time to snatch theirs. Rathe ordered them into the center.

They were just in time. Three men hadn't made it. The things flew among them, hurling themselves at the interlocked shields, battering with spiked claws.

Rathe had no more time for orders. He was fighting for his life. The creatures looked like giant spiked insects, armored in glistening black chitin. His sword glanced off a carapace, clipped off a waving antenna. The thing facing him hissed in pain and backed off. Another took its place, mandibles snapping. Rathe counted at least a dozen of the monsters. He sliced with his sword, and the thing ducked under the blow. Next to him Dren stepped forward, shouting inarticulately, bringing his blade down hard on its head. The carapace cracked, splattering them both with steaming black ichor.

One landed on top of the shield wall. Rathe gave a yell and pushed it off — they didn't weigh that much! — and it fell to the ground, off balance. He overturned it with a savage kick, then stabbed down, his blade cutting through the intricate red pattern that marked its underside. The thing jerked and died. Rathe grinned wolfishly. Even death could die!

But the battle still hung by a thread. Next to him, Dren

screamed hideously. His sword arm had been caught by the huge black pincers. Dren staggered back, blood pumping from the stump of his wrist. A gap opened in the shield wall. The creature moved in.

Shieldless, Tam stepped forward, lunging for its chest. Her blade sank deep — and stuck. It jerked back, tearing it from her grasp. Without sword or shield, Tam was defenseless. Rathe whirled and brought his shield edge smashing down on the thing's neck. There was a snap and the mutant clattered to the ground, limbs sprawling. But he had neglected the foe in front of him. A heavy weight crashed into him and a spiked claw smashed into his face. A sharp pain, a taste of blood. And everything went dark.

Rathe walked through a huge echoing space, as dark as death. At first he thought he floated in the night, but the slippery floor was solid under him, and he realized it was night-black stone. The stars were lamps, glittering above a dais or — was it an altar? He was in a vast columned hall. And someone was calling his name. A woman's voice, a woman's scent. Familiar. His mother?

The voice turned to laughter in his mind, not mocking, but gentle. A woman. His lover? His daughter?

"Everything," said the woman. "And yet, nothing. Can you see it? Are you strong enough, keen enough?"

There was a pattern etched in the glass floor — fine lines that caught the light of the lamps, that glittered, gleaming dully. With a start, he realized that he was following it. He looked, and saw that at the end was a doorway. An arch.

The lines flared up. They formed a shape. A word? No, more than that. A complex design. A symbol. A rune. Strange, intricate. And somehow, like the female voice, familiar.

Rathe realized he had to follow the shape on the floor, the rune, to the door at the end... but he was so tired.

"You are dying, Rathe. You must live. Muster your strength. Follow the path. Open the door."

Rathe struggled forward, toward the door. He lifted one leg, then the other. He felt so tired.

"Can you help?" he asked the voice.

"Only if you reach me," she said. "I am bound Outside." And

there was a note of sadness that tore at Rathe's heart. "You must help yourself, Rathe... and then help me, if you survive."

"Who are you?"

"I am the one who hid herself," said the voice. She sounded tired, desperate. "Rathe, I must trick him. Run!"

Then the room began to shake. Rathe looked about, widely. The great columns began to sway. Rocks were falling from the ceiling.

Rathe ran, instinctively following the pattern of the rune. A chunk of ceiling cracked and fell, missing him by a few feet. He slipped and nearly fell as the floor shook, but kept his balance.

Rathe ran, and the door seemed to get no closer. A lamp swayed and shattered. Fire splashed the hall. The lamps went out.

Rathe ran, and the sound of breaking glass was all around him. Ahead of him a crack was forming in the heaving floor, in front of the bright doorway. He ran, and the crack began to enlarge, splitting the rune in two. The gap widened in front of Rathe. He leaped...

Chapter Two

"Rathe."

Someone was calling his name. A woman's voice. But it wasn't *her* voice.

"Rathe!"

Everything was shaking. But he had escaped. Followed the rune...

No. *He* was being shaken. His eyes opened.

"Rathe, can you hear me?"

"I'm awake," he said. Rathe realized he was lying on a wooden bed. Tam was shaking him. Light was shining through a barred window, illuminating her face. He smiled at her, glad to see she was unhurt, although she looked tired and worried.

"You're all right!" Tam said. "I thought you'd lie there till the gods returned!" She matched his smile and some of the worry lines vanished, but her eyes had a haunted look that Rathe had never seen there before.

"How long was I out? An hour?" Rathe said hoarsely. He coughed. His throat was dry.

"A day and a night," Tam said. "This is the fourth hour after noon." She looked away. "We thought we'd lost you."

That long? Rathe thought. He looked around the room. Rough timber walls. A simple bed. A small window. A pair of candles on a low table. Where was this?

"We're back in Fort Thunder," Tam said. "The west guard tower."

Rathe realized he had spoken aloud. Fort Thunder was a small wooden stockade, one of many built to protect loggers during Stonekeep's seasonal forays into the Vale of Khera. The huge logging expeditions wouldn't be here until the fall equinox — a month away. Until then, they were the fort's sole occupants.

He wanted to ask Tam what was going on, but he felt dizzy and light-headed. His throat felt like a desert. "Water," Rathe croaked.

"Right away." She left.

A day and a night? Rathe tried to bring himself up to date. The last thing he remembered was a spiked claw slamming into his head. And then he'd been elsewhere — and something had happened. A dream?

The woman's voice in his mind. The great rune, burning and broken in the huge temple hall.

Temple? Why did he think that? But it fit, somehow.

Rathe touched his head. A cloth bandage was wrapped around it. It felt tender.

Fort Thunder. Hoth's patrol had been garrisoning the outpost when Orvig had arrived with orders to search for the missing Seth party. Memories flooded back. The battle. Whispering Death. Hoth's death. The others. He had taken command, but so many had been hurt or killed. How many had made it? At least Tam was still there. Rathe felt a sudden swell of affection for her. Had she died... If they been anything but officer and soldier, Rathe felt they could have shared a deeper relationship. As it was, he valued her comradeship — and tried not to think of might-have-beens.

There was a tap on the door and Rathe brought his thoughts back down to earth. It was Tam, her helmet filled with water.

"From the well," she explained. She eyed him. "You look better."

"Ah." He propped himself up and drank it gratefully, then splashed some over his face. "That feels good."

"You look better," Tam agreed. "Welcome back to the living."

"Thank you," Rathe said. Then he asked the question that was on his mind. "Who did we lose, Tam? I saw Hoth fall, and Warren."

Tam looked grim. "They got Kaja too," she replied. "She never even had time to draw her sword."

"What about Orvig?"

Tam shook her head. "The fates loved Orvig that day. He was caught in the open at first, but none of the creatures touched him." She shrugged. "Maybe they don't like the taste of dwarf."

Orvig was alive! "Who else? Did Dren make it?"

"No." Tam sighed. "He bled to death. We lost Calvert. Nam too. It was only a flesh wound, but the poison..."

Rathe shook his head. So many dead. "Poison?"

"On their spikes." Tam took a deep breath, sat down on the bed beside him. Rathe realized she was exhausted. "That's how we almost lost you. Some got into your wound."

Nam. Calvert. Dren. They'd all fallen after he took command. Maybe he should have done something else, some plan that would have saved them. Only five of them were left. Tam, Loric, Quin, Orvig, and himself. "So few left..."

Tam gripped Rathe's shoulder. "They struck so fast. Hoth first. Kaja and Warren never knew what hit them. After Hoth went down, I thought we were dead — I couldn't even find my shield, they were everywhere. But you took command, got us into the shield wall. Until then, I didn't think we'd make it." Tam pulled him around to face her. "You saved us, Rathe," she finished.

Rathe shook his head. "It was the girl," he told Tam. "She said her name was Kel. She warned us." If there had only been himself and Dren awake, we wouldn't have made it, Rathe realized. They owed her their lives. But who was she?

"Dren mentioned her, before he died," Tam said. She sounded curious. "Said a savage woman warned you?"

"Yes," Rathe said. "At least, she was dressed like a savage. She wore skins." He tried to picture her face, and it came to him easily: a striking face framed with black curly hair, and flashing green eyes. Would he see her again? "I wish I knew who she was," he said.

"Well, whatever she was, I'm glad for her warning," Tam said. "We wouldn't have made it otherwise. If we'd been asleep..." she shivered. "What did she call them? Whispering Death."

Rathe glanced out the tower's barred window. He could see the walls of the fort, and beyond it, the dark forests of Khera Vale. "You've got guards posted?" Rathe asked.

"Yes," Tam answered. "We broke out the javelins from the fort's store. But I'm keeping everyone inside, as a precaution."

"Good." Rathe heaved himself up to a sitting position. "How many of the creatures did we kill?"

"We got five of them," Tam said. "The others fled. No sign of them since. I hope they stay away until the gods return."

Rathe nodded thoughtfully. They had killed five. Perhaps six or seven had fled. Once surprise was lost, the Whispering Death wouldn't fight human soldiers one-to-one. But if there were more of the monsters... staying here would be foolhardy, and Stonekeep would have to be warned.

There was a knock on the door.

"Enter," said Tam and Rathe, simultaneously. They looked at each other. Tam gave a faint grin. She'd been in command for a whole day now. It seemed to agree with her.

The door opened. It was Loric. He was holding his helmet and wasn't wearing armor, but he had his sword buckled on and his shield slung over his back. There was a bruise on his temple, but he seemed to have gotten through the fight in one piece.

The young soldier broke into a grin. "Glad to see you up, sir," Loric said. He cleared his throat, but Rathe thought he looked healthier than on the march. Loric turned to Tam. "Orvig sent me. He says there's something he wants to show you. But I don't think he's in a hurry. Can I get you anything to eat, sir?"

Rathe looked inquisitively at Tam.

"Quin's in the kitchens. He made stew. I've already eaten."

"Sounds good," Rathe said. He realized he was hungry.

"Tell Orvig we'll be there soon," Tam told Loric. The man nodded and left, then returned a few minutes later with a bowl of stew, two slices of bread and a pitcher of water. Quin served them, then excused himself.

"I thought we were low on rations," Rathe said, dipping his bread into the stew. "This is delicious."

"We used the monsters," Tam said. "They cook up good."

Rathe choked, staring at her in amazement. Then he realized Tam was grinning at him.

"Vegetables from the storeroom," she said, wiping spattered soup off the table. "Really."

Rathe laughed. He felt a bit better, knowing Tam could still joke. He finished the stew and rose to his feet. He was a bit shaky, but the dizziness was gone. "I'd like to inspect the fort," he told Tam. "Then let's go see what Orvig's found out."

He found his sword and shield, and together they left the room and climbed downstairs. Tam had chosen the west guard tower as their refuge.

"With only five of us, I didn't want to try to cover the whole fort," Tam explained.

"It's a good choice," Rathe approved. But it was also a good trap, he realized. They couldn't stay here forever. "Where's Orvig?"

"South barracks. Follow me."

Tam led him into the fort's open courtyard. The air was cool, and Rathe couldn't help but glance nervously at the sky. The overcast of the last few days had broken at last, and now only a few white clouds drifted amid the blue expanse. It seemed peaceful. It had probably seemed peaceful to Hoth, before he died. Fort Thunder was a sturdy structure, but Rathe knew its thick wooden walls would avail little against the Whispering Death. The fort's builders hadn't expected winged foes.

They crossed the courtyard and ducked back inside, entered the south barracks hall. Rathe wrinkled his nose. Something smelled peculiar. Acrid, bitter...

Orvig met him at the door. Rathe knelt and gathered his stepfather into a hug.

"Well, boy," Orvig said gruffly, when he had pulled free. "Finished your beauty sleep?"

"I think so," Rathe said. He looked the dwarf over, noticing the dark circles under his eyes. "You look like you could use some sleep yourself."

"Can't sleep," Orvig said. His eyes narrowed. "Work to do."

Jhen, Rathe thought.

"No, I'm fine, boy," said Orvig, as if reading Rathe's expression. "But I promised your father I'd take better care of you, and then you go making me a liar." He peered up at Rathe's bandaged head. "It's a miracle ye survived the poison."

"I know," said Rathe. "I had... help."

Orvig raised an eyebrow.

"We'll speak of it later," Rathe said. "Now tell me what you've learned." He motioned Tam over, from where she'd been standing by the door.

"Take a look at these." The table was covered with a stained cloth. Upon it lay two of the Whispering Death. One was nearly intact, save for a hole in its eye. The other's carapace had been sliced open, its organs displayed. A scatter of knives and bottles covered the table top, next to a jug of water. A roll of parchment lay on the table, covered with sketches. The dwarf had been busy.

"Orvig had us bring two of them back," Tam said.

"Aye." Orvig said. "If you don't know your enemy, you're a fool."

Armored in glittering black and green chitin, the thing was too long and graceful to be a beetle. The forelegs were covered with deadly spikes. The head was dominated by giant mandibles and glittering multi-faceted compound eyes. Antennae quivered above it.

"It looks like a praying mantis," Tam said.

Rathe agreed. He'd seen the hungry little hunters sunning themselves on Stonekeep's walls during the summer. But those had been only a few inches long. This creature was seven feet from head to tail. The scary thing was, it was almost beautiful.

"Whispering Death," he said out loud. He searched for the name the girl had used.

"Orvig, have you ever heard of anything like it?"

The dwarf tugged on his beard. "The Deep Library of Stonekeep might have records of such things. Or... or Jhen might know. But our clan is the Stonemelters, lad. We deal in chemical reactions, not in bugs and mutants."

"Does that mean you don't know what it is?" Tam said. She prodded it with her sword-tip. Orvig slapped her hand away.

"It means I will have to find out," Orvig said. "When we found the hill on which Seth died, we had questions. Did such as these —" he tapped the creature's head with his knife "— slay the Seth party?"

"Who can doubt it?" said Rathe.

"Not I," the dwarf answered. "But remember the question we asked on the hill? If they were killed by mere creatures, what happened to their goods and weapons? And where did the sword-wounds come from, on the mules? Those questions remained unanswered."

"You said remained," Rathe said. He kept his patience. Orvig's lectures were something he had gotten used to in childhood.

"Aye, lad. Turn the intact creature over."

Rathe hesitated, reluctant to touch the Death without gloves. Then he obeyed. The thing was light and brittle, cool to the touch, but dry rather than slimy.

Tam leaned in closer to see, wrinkling her nose.

"What's that on its belly?" she asked.

It was a mark of some sort, a complex pattern in red, like a double hourglass.

"I've seen that mark before," Rathe said. He withdrew his hand. "On the one I killed." Memory of sudden terror as the Whispering Death's weight landed on his shield, a desperate thrust to dislodge it, the sword stabbing down as it thrashed on its back. "Is this the same one?"

"No," said Orvig. "All of them have it."

"So what?" said Tam. "The trailspider that bit my cousin Tara had a red diamond on its back." She pursed her lips. "Lots of poisonous insects have marks."

"Ah," said Orvig. "But not like this." He dipped his finger in the jug of water, then touched the mark, rubbed it. It smeared.

"Dye?" Rathe asked.

Orvig sniffed it. "Blood," he said gravely. "Drawn in blood."

Rathe sat down. This changed things. "Could the things be intelligent?" he finally asked. "Perhaps use this as war paint or something?"

"I doubt it," Orvig said. "I've dissected them. We, (and Rathe knew he meant the dwarves) know that the brain is the seat of thought. This thing has no more brain than a dog. I think they are clever, but not as much as a man." He caught Rathe's gaze, held it. "No, boy. Some intelligence is directing them."

Rathe stared at the bloody pattern on the creature. Something he remembered... "It looks like a rune," he finally said.

"It is indeed," Orvig answered, surprised. He gave Rathe a long glance. "How did you know?"

"My dream, I think." Rathe said.

"Go on," said Orvig. Tam nodded.

"While I was unconscious, I dreamed of a rune carved in black glass. A magickal symbol."

"It's magick?" Tam said. She drew back from the table.

Rathe understood Tam's unease. Long centuries ago, magick had been the driving force behind human society — and human warfare. Two rival cabals, the Lord Sorcerers of Atlantis and the Dark Warlocks of Ys, had warred with spells as well as steel. The final struggle had been an exchange of ever-more-deadly sorceries. The final spell had been cast by the Dark Warlocks. It went out of control, and the result was the Devastation: the end of the world.

Almost.

Continents burned, oceans boiled, and both warring nations sank beneath the waves. Even the gods had not escaped unscathed. Neither the Dark Warlocks nor the Lord Sorcerers survived — nor had most of the rest of humanity. The scattered survivors had taken centuries to rebuild human civilization, even with the help of the subterranean Dwarves. Other races were hit even harder — if the greenskinned throgs and their smaller cousins, the shargas, had been civilized before the Devastation, they were no longer. And none of the legendary Elves and few of the magick-using Faeries had been seen since the skies burned.

Since then, magick had been rightly feared. Among the humans and Dwarves of Stonekeep, only a few elder Magickians retained any knowledge of the old ways. Their rune magicks were a closely guarded secret, passed to trusted disciples, to be used only for the safety of the Keep itself.

Or so Rathe had always been taught.

"Magick," repeated Tam. "Right. I'll check on Loric and Quin."

Rathe nodded. "Do so," he said. She saluted, her gaze lingering on him for a second, then turned and left. Rathe saw the effort she made to straighten her shoulders as she strode away.

Magick. Here, among them, trying to kill them. Rathe knew he should be frightened, but instead he was fascinated. When Tam was gone, he turned to Orvig. "What could the rune be for?"

"Runes are the heart of magick," said Orvig slowly. "That much I know. There are other kinds of sorcery — rituals and such, or Elf magick — but they were lost in the Devastation. Rune magick is made by scribing the rune you want to use on a rune-item, like a staff or a wand, or even a sword. It stores the energy that powers the spell. But the nature of the spell is in the lines of the rune."

"But what does *this* rune mean?" Rathe asked eagerly. "Could it control the creatures?"

"That seems a likely truth."

"But who could have drawn it?"

"That I cannot say," Orvig said. "Each race has its own runes. I can read some dwarf runes, and recognize others, though I have not the art of magick. But this is not dwarf magick."

"Who else uses magickal runes?"

"The savage throgs have their shamans," Orvig said, "although their small cousins, the shargas, have no such art. And the tiny Faeries use runes as well, though neither man nor dwarf from Stonekeep has seen their kind in many a year. And your own race, of course. Aye, human runes are mighty."

Orvig peered down at the design drawn in blood. "It might be a human rune," he said. "I know too little of your race's magick. Human spell-crafters are secretive, just as are the Dwarves', of course." Orvig sighed. "Knowledge should not be hoarded, but suspicion and secrecy still breed ignorance, even after centuries of cooperation. No, I cannot say for sure."

"The rune was drawn in blood," Rathe observed. He thought for a moment. "Could the blood have some significance? Perhaps drive the creatures to attack things?"

Orvig nodded. "That could be it. Blood has power, certainly. And ...."

"Wait," Rathe interrupted. A terrible thought had struck him. If blood had power...

"Tam said the Whispering Death didn't attack you."

"The lass spoke true," Orvig said. The dwarf frowned casting his thoughts back to the battle. "One of them flew right past me, though I was nearest it, and had no shield. I wondered why..."

"It fits!" Rathe said. "If the rune was drawn in *human* blood. The things attacked humans, not dwarves, not animals. Humans."

"You're not saying the dwarves had anything to do with this?" Orvig's tone was low, but his eyes flashed.

"No, of course not," Rathe said. "But think of this: if they were magicked to attack only humans, they couldn't have eaten your sister. Jhen might still be alive!"

"Aye!" The dwarf's face cracked into a grin. "That could be. That could be." He suddenly frowned. "You'll be planning on returning to the Keep with the soldiers, to report?"

"I want to find her as much as you," Rathe said. "But Stonekeep has to know."

"Aye. But I'll not go back without Jhen," Orvig said slowly. His stared at the floor. "Not if she may be alive. My duty to family and clan demands it."

"You can't search for her alone."

"*She's* alone. Ah, well." With an effort, the dwarf wrenched his thoughts back to the creatures. "But there are other mysteries." He tapped the table with his knife. "Tell me," Orvig said. "What did you mean when you spoke of seeing a rune in your dream?"

"At first I thought I was floating..." Rathe began.

He told the dwarf of the columned hall with its floor of black glass, the feminine voice that spoke to him, and the rune in the floor he had followed even as it had shattered...

Orvig listened intently. "Was the rune in the dream the same as the runes on the insect?" he said at last.

Rathe shook his head. "No. Similar... but the shattered rune was far more complex, more — powerful. Complete." He visualized the rune, then pointed to the symbol drawn on the creature. "This is like a sentence, ripped from a page, or a single line from a poem. Does that make sense?"

Orvig nodded encouragingly. Rathe went on.

"But the rune I saw — it felt like it was connected to the woman's voice, somehow, almost like it was her name. Yet it also seemed somehow familiar. Like a childhood memory." Rathe looked up, met Orvig's gaze. "And when the rune shattered, I felt like — " he struggled for words, "— like something inside me had broken as well." He shook his head. "It's silly, isn't it?"

"I have paper and quill," said Orvig. "Can you draw me this rune?"

"I can see it in my mind," Rathe said. "I'll try."

He was no artist, but several attempts and much spattered ink later, Rathe had a depiction that looked right.

"You're very quiet," Rathe told Orvig. It was true. The dwarf was simply staring at it. "Do you recognize it?"

Orvig nodded, his expression unreadable. Rathe watched as he fished into his belt pouch and pulled out a ring. The dwarf held it out. The band was of heavy gold. A black stone glittered on it.

"It's beautiful," Rathe said. "But — have I seen it before?" It felt familiar. "Where is it from? What is the stone?"

"Obsidian," said Orvig said. "Volcanic glass. Like, I would guess, the floor in your dream. He held it into the light. "Look at the glass. Look closely."

The light caught the jewel, revealed a tracery of fine lines carved on its face.

"The rune in the temple!" Rathe exclaimed. "But where — ?"

"It's your mother's ring," Orvig said simply. He offered it. "Here, take it. Put it on."

Rathe accepted the ring numbly, his thoughts in turmoil. His mother, his father — he had never known them. A week after his first birthday, both had left the Keep... never to return. He knew his father Clave had been a logger and later a soldier, that his mother Rhea had been a healer. He had been raised by Orvig. When he grew older, he had learned that his father had once saved Orvig's life, that a mutual debt of friendship existed between them. His adoption had been Orvig's way of repaying that debt, but in time, bonds of genuine affection had grown between the dwarf and the human child.

"How can this be?" Rathe asked. He held the ring in his palm, weighing it. It was surprisingly heavy. "I don't understand."

"Aye, nor do I, boy," said Orvig. "Not entirely. But knowledge aids understanding. And I have kept you in the dark too long." He took a drink of water. "I know you have questions. Ask."

"How did you get the ring? What does it have to do with my father?"

"Little to do with your father," said Orvig. "Save that he would not abandon your mother."

"What do you mean?"

The dwarf almost seemed not to hear the question. He shook his head slowly, and his reply was no reply at all, but another question. "What do you know of the gods?" Orvig asked.

"Only what you taught me, what everyone knows," Rathe answered, surprised. "That beings called Light and Darkness created the universe. They were the Eldest Gods. When they created Earth, they gave birth to the Younger Gods, men, Dwarves, everyone. Then they went away."

"Correct," Orvig said. "But what of the Younger Gods?"

"There are ten," Rathe said impatiently. "One for each of the heavenly spheres. Khull-Khuum, who is the sun. Helion, the nearest to its fires. Aquila, the evening star. Thera, that is the Earth. Azrael, who is the red planet. Marif, the world of many moons. Safrinni, the ringed planet. And Yoth-soggoth and Ko-soggoth, the unseen pair." Rathe grinned. "Unseen until your kin showed us how to grind lenses to make telescopes."

Orvig nodded, pleased. His clan, the Chuk'li, or Stonemelters, made many of the strong acids used in lenscrafting.

"But what has any of this to do with my parents?"

"Patience, boy. Where are the gods now?" Orvig countered.

"The Devastation happened." Rathe said. "There was a war among the gods, echoing the war of men. Khull-Khuum, the Shadow King, betrayed his brothers and sisters. Some fought, or tried to escape, but they weren't strong enough, and the Shadow King trapped their essences in mystic orbs. Only the goddess Thera did not waste her energy trying to flee or battle him. Instead, she worked her own magick to change his spell. So when they were trapped, the orbs that held them flew from Khull-Khuum's grip, and escaped into the heavens. And forever after..." Rathe paused, and looked Orvig in the eye, "...forever after, they now orbit the sun, remaining just outside his grasp. All of which every child knows."

Angrily, Rathe slammed his fist on the table, sending the glass bottles and jugs dancing. "Tell me! What does it have to do with this ring and my mother? And why didn't you tell me about the ring?"

"Aye, you have a right to be angry, maybe," Orvig said. "But I made a promise to your father..." He paused, as if unsure how to continue. "All right. As you say, the Younger Gods were bound in the orbs, all save the Shadow King. But though they have little power, these imprisoned gods are still worshipped by a few folk, who keep the ancient faith alive and hope for their return."

"When the Gods return," Rathe quoted. "But it's just a saying. Almost no one follows the old faith any more."

"*Almost* no one," agreed Orvig. "Your mother was an exception." He looked at Rathe. "She was a priestess of Thera, boy, strong in her faith, a healer and maybe more. She came here from another Keep, I think. Perhaps she sought converts. In any case, she found one: your father, Clave. Or perchance it was simply love that made him follow her way, for they soon married."

"What happened to her?" Rathe asked quietly. He had known his mother was different, but few of his father's age would talk about her. He had always assumed she had been disliked, or simply distrusted as an outlander from another Keep. Now he wondered if it had been something more than that.

"When you were a year and a month old, Rhea had a vision of some sort," Orvig said. "I don't know the details, only what your father told me: that she felt a calling and heeded it." He sighed. "And whatever road she took, she could not risk an infant there. She begged Clave to stay behind and rear you. But he would not leave her side. Where they journeyed, I cannot say."

"They left me behind."

"They did not want to take you into danger," Orvig corrected him softly. "I still recall the last words Rhea said to me: 'I ask you to keep Rathe safe until we return, and I ask this favor not just as a parent, but as priestess.' And then she gave me her ring, saying, 'He is the last of the old blood. If I fail, then his time may come.' But your father said 'Pray it does not.'" Orvig shook his head. "I knew he didn't want you following them on some wild quest before you were ready. Then Rhea kissed you, and they left Stonekeep, and vanished into the forest. I never saw them again. No doubt they died in the outlands."

Rathe nodded. He looked at the ring, then slipped it into his pocket and left the room. Outside, the clouds were already stained red by the setting sun.

Although he was tired and his wound was starting to ache, Rathe took the time to inspect the defenses Tam had erected. They seemed sound enough. Since the Whispering Death seemed nocturnal (they hoped) they would all spend the night in the West Tower, with the gates shut, windows barricaded and weapons at hand. One person would always be awake, and a fire would be lit at all times, with torches ready.

Dusk came quickly. The surviving soldiers and Orvig took their meal together — more of Quin's stew — and prepared to sleep. Quin had first watch.

"Hope those cursed mutants fear flame," said Loric. He waved a torch skeptically and shook his head.

"Most animals do," Rathe said. He forced a grin. "Singe their wings right off."

Loric nodded. "Maybe so."

"Try to get some sleep."

"Goodnight, sir," said Quin, echoed by Tam and Loric. Orvig sat on a bench in the corner. The dwarf had said he'd take the first watch with Quin. Rathe had volunteered to stand an ordinary watch, but Tam — and the others — had convinced him otherwise.

"You're in command, boy," Orvig had said. "But you were half dead. You'll need your wits about you tomorrow, runes or no runes, when we sorry fools want to know what to do. Now sleep!"

Rathe curled up in his blanket. There was little left of the night, and Rathe was not sure he could sleep. He knew he had to make a decision. Should they return to Stonekeep, and report the creatures — the Whispering Death? Or hunt for Jhen — and, Rathe admitted, try to find the mysterious green-eyed woman? Kel. The woman he owed his life to.

He glanced up from his blanket out the window, where Quin stood guard. A full moon stared back, surrounded by the autumn stars.

He would sleep on it.

Chapter Three

Rathe woke to Loric's hand shaking his shoulder.

"Time to get up, sir," the soldier said.

Rathe sat up. He was well rested. His head still felt tender, but aside from that, it was the first proper night's sleep — in a bed — he'd had in nearly a week.

The dim light of early morning was coming from the barred window of the tower. Around him the others were waking up, struggling into their tunics and boots. The tower smelled of sweat and cooking vegetables.

"That was a rough night," Tam was saying to Quin. She glared meaningfully at Loric. "'Least I don't snore like a kettle."

"Not much loss," Quin grumbled. "Kept tossing and turning. I hardly got any sleep. Rune magick drawn in blood! How can we fight that?"

How indeed? Rathe thought. But he kept silent.

As he waited for breakfast, Rathe studied the map of Khera Vale. It had been prepared by Stonekeep's master cartographer. Tam had salvaged it from Hoth's body.

"You have any dreams, boy?" Orvig asked. He was stirring the stew pot.

"No," Rathe answered absently, and then realized he *had* dreamed. And suddenly, it came back to him. "Well, yes. I saw the broken rune again," he said softly.

"Aye? Anything else?" Orvig asked curiously.

"Maybe. No voices. But a feeling of... I don't know. Wanting? Incompleteness?" He looked at his finger. He was wearing his mother's ring. "That's strange," Rathe said.

"What, dreaming of it?" Orvig shook his head. "Hardly, boy. We were talking of the rune until late. I'd be surprised if you didn't."

"No, not the dream, the ring," Rathe said. He tugged it off, weighed it in his palm. "It's just that I had tied it around my neck. I don't remember putting it on. Oh well," he shrugged, and slipped it back on his finger. It fit well, and he liked its feel.

Rathe turned back to the map, spreading it out on the table. Fort Thunder was clearly marked, the last outpost on a logging trail that led back south toward Stonekeep. But the same trails also led north and east, deeper into the forest, past the hill where Seth's party had fallen, to within a few miles of the savage villages of Adra and Gothmeg — barbarous names Rathe had trouble pronouncing. Rathe knew that Seth had hoped to visit them, then perhaps press on to trade for furs and hides with tribes that had never been encountered before.

Further east and north, the map was mostly white space, but Rathe had heard the forest called Khera Vale stretched eastward, gradually giving way to broken badlands and, eventually, the foothills of the mountains called the Shadow's Teeth.

At the moment, though, the problem was closer at hand. Rathe traced the route between Fort Thunder and Stonekeep, mentally adding miles and days. Then his finger drifted northward.

After breakfast, Rathe rolled up the map and gathered the three soldiers and Orvig about him. "I've made a decision," he said.

Eight ears pricked up.

"I know you've all heard what Orvig found on the mutant insects — the Whispering Death. Runes. That means magick is involved." He paused to let that sink in. "The runes are drawn in blood. I think they're controlling the creatures. Making them attack our folk, but not animals — or even other races like the Dwarves."

Except for Orvig, everyone nodded.

"We've got a problem," Rathe said. "Stonekeep needs to know about this, soon. Before they send anyone else into the Vale unprepared for the creatures."

"We whipped 'em good enough once we knew what we were dealing with," said Quin belligerently.

"That we did," said Rathe delicately. It was an exaggeration, but good for morale. "But if they're taken by surprise like Seth's party," (and us, he mentally added) "they'll be ambushed and slaughtered."

"We have to get word back home," Tam agreed. "But what about the dwarf's sister?" She flicked a glance at Orvig. "If the bugs only eat our kind, she might still be alive."

"It's possible," Rathe replied. "We can't be sure."

"Gods!" said Tam. "We're not sure about *anything*. We've lost half the patrol and we still don't even know who sent those things after us!"

"Maybe that girl the Watch-Second saw?" said Loric.

"Nah," said Quin. "Why would she warn us?"

"Right," said Rathe. "You're right, Tam, Quin. There's too much Stonekeep needs to find out. That's why we'll split up. Tam, you'll take Loric and Quin, and carry word back home. Orvig and I will scout the forest, see if Hoth was right and if the savage tribes are on the move..."

"Wait a minute," said Tam. She leaned over the table. "You're going into the forest alone? We should go with you."

There was a chorus of muted agreement from the other two men. But Rathe shook his head.

"Getting word of the creatures back to Stonekeep is just as important as finding answers. As Tam said, we've two duties. To find out what killed Hoth and the others. But also, to warn the Keep." He unrolled the map, motioned Tam over. "Here we are." His finger

stabbed Fort Thunder. "And there's Stonekeep. It's a two-day journey south, but if you move fast and light you might be able to make it
in a day and a half. I'll take Orvig and strike northeast, toward the villages here. We'll see if we can find any connection between the savages and the killer mutants."

"Orvig's no soldier," Tam said. "I am. I should go with you."

Rathe shook his head. "You're next in command after me. I
need you in charge. Orvig may not be a warrior, but he knows the
forests," and Rathe smiled grimly, "and if he tastes bad to the bugs, I
won't be taking him into any more danger than you'll face." He rose
to his feet. "No more questions. We march in an hour."

They made their preparations and divided the supplies they
could carry, Rathe making sure each of them had three javelins and a
torch besides their normal kit. Afterwards, Rathe took Tam aside.

"I'm depending on you to get through," Rathe told her. "Those
things may still be out there. Keep a fire at night, just in case. They
found us easily enough in the dark last time."

"You just take care of yourself," said Tam. "I'll manage Loric
and Quin." She stared out into the forest depths. "I'm going home.
You're going deeper into the Vale."

"We'll be careful," Rathe said. "I might even be able to link up
with you in a day or so, if we don't find anything. But if I don't make
it back in time, try to convince the council not to do anything rash."

"Huh. I'm no speaker."

"Just tell them what happened," Rathe said. "You'll do fine."

"I still don't like it," Tam said. "Be careful, Rathe."

"You too," said Rathe. "See you in Stonekeep."

They clasped hands, and then Tam turned away. "In Stonekeep,"
she said. "Loric, Quin — let's move out."

Rathe and Orvig set out to the northeast, following the trail.
The mud had dried out, making walking easier, and the weather
remained good, neither warm nor cool. The forest didn't seem especially dangerous in the morning light, but each of them kept a wary
eye on the sky. So far, the Whispering Death had struck twice at

night, but what did that prove?

Morning was fading to afternoon when they reached the grassy knoll where the creatures had attacked them. Orvig had told him that the bodies of Hoth and the other soldiers lay in a single shallow grave, marked only by a small standing stone with their names scratched on it. Rathe decided not to visit it; there was nothing there for him.

"Aye," Orvig agreed. "We've dug too many graves lately." He shrugged. Their mood was grim, and they spoke little. Although neither would speak of it, each feared the coming of night.

They circled the battlefield, and pressed on, but only half a mile away, Rathe stopped. "Oh, gods," he said slowly. "Take a look at this."

"Tracks?" said Orvig. His voice was eager: he was glad to be looking for Jhen.

"Not tracks," Rathe said.

Orvig stepped forward over a fallen log, and brushed a hanging spiderweb out of his face. He peered down where Rathe was pointing. It was a empty snakeskin, dry, white and harmless — but the snake that had shed it would have been easily twenty feet long.

Rathe examined the skin. It seemed fairly fresh — at least, it did not fall apart at his touch. The pattern was complex, huge diamonds alternating with stripes. He had never seen anything like it.

Each man looked at each other.

"Giant snakes," Orvig finally said. "Fine, boy. Oh, fine." He shook his head, as if it was Rathe's fault. They moved on, but this time, they watched the underbrush as well as the sky.

A few minutes down the trail, Rathe had an irresistible thought. He turned, grinning, and clapped a grumbling Orvig on the shoulder.

"Maybe they eat giant insects," he said cheerfully.

After a few more miles of hard marching, they found a likely campsite near a rocky outcropping that Rathe hoped would be defensible, and began gathering deadwood for a fire. That night, they took turns standing watch. But despite Rathe's fears, nothing more lethal than mosquitoes assailed them, nor did he remember any more strange dreams. They broke camp early the next day.

Soon they passed the hill where the Seth party had fallen, and by mid-afternoon had penetrated deep into the forest, where the cedar and juniper trees grew thick, almost obscuring the faint trail. Hoth's map was now nearly useless: Rathe had little idea how far they had traveled. They had long since left Stonekeep's logging trails: now they followed other tracks, made, they guessed, by deer, or possibly by savages themselves. It was late in the day, and only faint shafts of sunlight pierced the wooded canopy.

Rathe's legs were beginning to ache. He thought of calling a halt and looking for a campsite, when he noticed that the trees seemed to thin ahead. Motioning Orvig forward, he brushed aside a tree branch — and found himself on the edge of a wide clearing. In the midst of it was a cluster of rude huts, surrounded by vegetable plots. There were fenced pens for pigs or fowl, and a well in the center of the village. And yet....

"There's no one here," Rathe decided. "Not even animals."

He didn't like the look of this deserted, silent village. With a start, he realized it reminded him of the hill where they had found Seth's party. There was no smell of death, but something felt wrong, very wrong. "Is this Adra or Goff... Goth... Goth-meg?"

"I think Adra, lad," said Orvig. He grimaced. "I'd expected to see smoke from their cook fires some time ago." He shook his head. "To speak truth, I'd been a bit worried we'd gotten lost and missed the place. But it's where it should be."

"Let's look around." Rathe loosened his sword. "But cautiously. There may still be someone here."

They walked slowly into the village — if you could call two dozen huts a village, Rathe thought — but no one challenged them. The only signs of life were a few dragonflies that buzzed lazily about, sunning themselves on fence posts. Adra's huts were of wattle and daub construction. To Rathe, used to the solidity of Stonekeep and the sturdy wood frontier forts, they seemed disturbingly fragile. Many of the buildings and fences were in poor repair, but whether the gaps and debris were from neglect, bad weather or deliberate vandalism neither could tell.

Rathe tugged at the door-blanket of the nearest hut. Nothing happened. He pulled the blanket aside and entered, ducking to pass through the low doorway. Inside, it smelled faintly of dung and charcoal. The floor was packed earth, with a firepit near the back. The only furniture was a wooden bench. On it stood two pottery jars. A third lay on the ground, broken into a dozen pieces. Kernels were scattered about it. Corn?

Rathe turned to survey the room — then jumped, as he saw staring eyes looking into his own. He stepped backward, bringing his weapon up, as the dwarf watched from outside in alarm. Then he laughed, seeing that the threatening faces were just painted wood.

"Only masks," he said, reaching above the doorframe to remove one.

"Masks?" Stepping hastily into the hut, Orvig slapped his hand away. Rathe drew back obediently, looking his puzzlement.

"Don't touch," the dwarf said grimly. He looked up, wincing as his neck popped. "These are spirit-masks."

"What do they do?"

"Jhen spoke of them once. The savages carve them when someone dies, leave them over the door for a month to keep the ghosts away. Touching one is bad luck, they say." He tugged his beard. "Three deaths in one house. Within a month. Not good at all."

The pair left the hut and entered its neighbor. Inside they found no signs of life or recent occupancy. But four spirit masks hung above the entrance.

The third hut they checked was the same.

"I don't like it," Rathe said, almost whispering. "Is everyone here dead?"

"Maybe so," said Orvig. "But if so, who made the masks?" He glanced at the position of the sun. "I think we should split up. If it's all the same to you, boy, I'd rather not be here by nightfall."

Rathe nodded. "You take the east end," he said. "I'll take the west. Be careful!"

Rathe moved from hut to hut, opening the blanket that covered each door, peering inside, sometimes entering. But in each, the story was the same. No sign of life, but no sign of death. Nothing at all, save the silent masks.

Orvig was getting frustrated. He'd searched a half-dozen huts, and the story was the same: Nothing. Oh, he'd found spirit masks a-plenty, broken pottery, ashes from fire pits, a broken hatchet. He wondered if Rathe had found anything.

He was beginning to think that the village had been deliberately looted. And yet, it was also tidy — as if someone had been through afterwards. Well, there was still one more hut to check.

He pushed his way past the hut's entrance and immediately noticed a faint pungent smell, as if something — fishes, perhaps — had been cooked there. Orvig allowed himself a faint smile. Perhaps the village wasn't deserted after all.

Rathe had found a pyramid of skulls.

They were stacked in a pigpen behind a hut on the western edge of the village: nearly a dozen skulls, a grisly monument of bleached white bone. In front, facing the forest, was planted a wooden pole or staff, about three feet long and a finger's breadth thick. Attached to it was a leather thong from which hung a spirit mask. The entire length of the pole was carved with runes.

Although the day was warm, Rathe shivered. Was he seeing the fate of Adra's villagers? But there weren't enough skulls...

Rathe climbed over the pen's fence and squinted at the runes on the staff. Some of the symbols seemed familiar: the middle one seemed like an abstracted version of the rune in his dream, on the ring he now wore. Others were totally unfamiliar. But felt drawn to them all. He had a sudden desire to touch the staff, to possess it — but the very strength of the feeling made him doubt it.

Everyone knew magick was treacherous.

There was something odd about the skulls, too. They seemed almost malformed... Gingerly, Rathe reached down and grasped one of the ivory domes, taking care not to unbalance the pyramid and bring them all down. He traced its texture with his fingers. It felt dry but curiously brittle. It was intact, showing no sign of damage, and

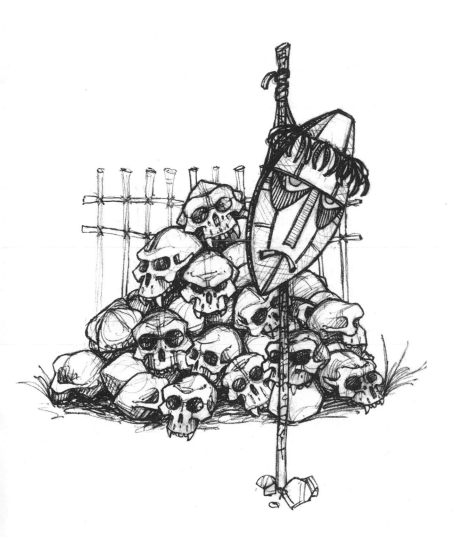

lighter than he thought it would be... but then, he had never held a human skull before.

Then he realized what was wrong. The slope of the forehead was subtly different, the jaw enlarged, the teeth pointed. *Not human,* Rathe realized. But far too large to be a sharga skull. Certainly not a dwarf. What did that leave? It had to belong to a throg.

He examined others. They were throg skulls, all right. That made him feel a bit better, but not much. What were they doing here, in a human village? Had the Whispering Death been here? Involuntarily, Rathe glanced at the sky. The sun was low and veiled in cloud, but dusk was still at least an hour away. The only living thing he saw was a distant bird — it looked like a hawk, or maybe even an eagle — wheeling over the forest. It was time to find Orvig, he decided. Maybe the dwarf would know what the skulls meant.

Then Rathe heard the sound. Was it a kind of rustling? Or slithering? It was behind him, on the other side of the nearest hut. Getting closer. A vision of the giant snakeskin popped into his mind. *Twenty feet long,* he thought. His sword whispered from its scabbard, and he crouched down, taking cover behind the pile of skulls.

Seconds passed like hours. Hunkered down, he waited for it to appear, darting quick glances over his shoulder. *Gods,* he thought. *What if it's gone after Orvig?* He heard a pebble move. Time to risk it. Moving slowly, so as not to alarm the snake, he peered around the pile.

And found himself staring into wide green eyes only inches from his own — and a long knife, thrusting for his heart!

As Orvig entered the hut, wood chips crunched softly underfoot. Shards of broken pottery, old fish bones and one leather sandal with a broken strap lay in the corner. A cloak made entirely of black feathers hung from a peg in the wall, next to a pair of dangling fish hooks. Suspended from the ceiling was a wicker cage imprisoning the tiny skeleton of a bird.

There were no spirit masks hanging above the entrance. That made sense to Orvig: this was clearly an abode of the living, not the dead. But it was strange, disturbing. To a dwarf, used to the tidy order of Stonekeep, the hut was chaos.

Orvig examined the room. A russet blanket was spread out in the middle of the room, and on it was spread the debris of a meal, fish bones, crumbs and nutshells. Ants scurried about, gathering them up. The hut reeked of burnt charcoal, fish, and herbal smells Orvig couldn't quite place. A single spear stood propped against the wall, just inside the entrance. Orvig hefted it experimentally: it was tipped with flint rather than iron, its ash shaft decorated with owl feathers, but the workmanship seemed good. Carved on the spear's blade were runes that even Orvig could recognize. They spelled death. Hurriedly, he put it back down.

Orvig nodded to himself. Herbs. Skeletons. Runes. The room *reeked* of magick.

Careful not to trip over the clutter, the dwarf stepped over a wooden wash tub — it was filled with dirty water — and plucked the bag from the stool. It was made of doeskin, drawn tight with a leather thong. He weighed it: it felt heavy, and he could feel several things inside. Stones?

He fumbled with the knot.

"Wait!" Rathe cried. He parried the thrust with his sword, then back-pedaled. "Kelandra, wait!"

"You!" the woman exclaimed. She stepped back, then slipped her knife into a belt sheath.

"Sorry," Rathe replied. He sheathed his own blade, feeling foolish. "I thought you were a snake."

"Oh, aye?" Kel said. She brushed sweat-soaked brown locks out of her eyes. "That what you were sneaking about for? I feared you'd try to stick me, and I'd have to spit you."

"I heard a snake nearby." Rathe said. "And we saw a big snake-skin a few miles away." He shrugged, feeling foolish. Twice, now, Kel had surprised him. At least this time she seemed nearly as startled as he was. "Stupid of me."

"Maybe," Kel said. "But maybe not. We get big ones in these parts, sure. Frightened you, did it? What did it look like?"

"Gray, like any snakeskin," Rathe said shortly. Somehow, he got the impression Kel was playing with him. "But it's not important." He gestured around him. "Is this your village?"

"I be Kelandra of Adra," she said formally. "And this" — and Rathe sensed an edge to her voice, "is Adra." She stepped forward and sat down on the pig-pen's fence, next to him. "And you are Rathe of Stonekeep, but I know little else. Save that I'm glad you still live."

Reflexively, Rathe touched his forehead. The wound still itched.

The young woman nodded. "You fell, and yet you survived. Be grateful. Few who bear the scars of the Whispering Death can say that."

"You saw our battle?" asked Rathe. He had supposed that she'd left after warning them.

"A little, from the forest's shelter. Heard more, though. I came back when the Tse'Mara were gone, saw your folk dragging you off. Still, better than I thought, you did." She favored him with a grim smile. "It was a good match."

"Many of us didn't make it," said Rathe. He gave her a challenging look. "Was it sport, to you?"

"Sport?" Kel was on her feet, eyes blazing. Her fingers curled around her knife.

"Wait," said Rathe hurriedly. "I meant no offense, lady. I know your warning saved many lives."

But the girl's temper crested as quickly as it had broken. "No," she said, sitting back down. "You have the right of it, Rathe. I should have helped, maybe, but one short blade would have been scant use in the storm of wings and iron. But as I said, your Keep-bred warriors did well enough — once you took over as war-chief." And this time she did smile, though it flickered across her face almost too fast to catch. Rathe liked what he saw. "Where are your warriors?" she asked.

She may have a nice smile, Rathe told himself, *but I know nothing about her.* "On patrol," he compromised. He cast for a question of his own. "But tell me. This village — Adra. Where is everyone, Kel?"

The woman's eyes narrowed. "Are you blind to the masks?" she exclaimed, "Less than a moon has passed, so their spirits still linger here."

"They're dead," Rathe guessed.

"Did I not say?" Kel replied. Her eyes burned dangerously, and Rathe felt an urge to back away. But instead, her hot gaze left him and turned inward. "My kin and clan. I carved the masks. Their remains I dragged to the hollow hills. The carrion that the Tse'Mara scorned to take. And each day, the masks ask me: what have *you* done, Kelandra? Why do you live?"

"I share your grief," Rathe said. He wanted to ask Kel how she survived. Instead, he extended his hand.

After a hesitation, Kel clasped it, her shoulders shaking. Her hand was slightly smaller than his own. "I..." she started to say. Then she froze.

"Kelandra?" Rathe looked around, up, wondering if she had spotted something.

"No, your ring," she said. She grasped his wrist, turned his hand over until she could see the gleaming black stone. "What is that rune?"

"It's a family heirloom." He shrugged, feeling reluctant to have to explain the dreams. "I wasn't wearing it last time. But tell me," he waved at the bone pyramid. "What are those skulls doing there? They're throgs, aren't they?"

Rathe was unprepared for the look of savage satisfaction that lit up Kel's face. "Une-Makhar warriors," she said, "who were careless."

"Une-Makhar?" The word meant nothing to Rathe.

Kel got up, began pacing back and forth. "A throg tribe from the broken lands to the north. But now they lay claim to the forest."

"Were they your people's enemies?" Rathe asked.

"No!" Kel said. She lowered her voice, but Rathe could feel the anger in it. "Not then, anyway. Some skirmishes, over the hunt, but some trade, also. We had a treaty. But a month ago, the Whispering Death came. I was gathering herbs in the wood. When I returned, all were dead. The creatures were feeding on the bodies."

"But what of the throgs?"

She gave a harsh laugh. "While the Tse'Mara fed, the throgs came, like maggots to a rotting corpse. Our hunters could have stood against the throgs, or fled into the forest and harried them. But against the Whispering Death, they fell. We all fell. All but me."

"Where did they come from?"

"The Death? Once they lived in the mountains, preying on small game and mountain goats. But now, someone controls them..."

"The rune underneath!" Rathe exclaimed.

"You saw that, did you?" said Kel. She gave him an appraising look. "Aye, the blood-rune."

"But why do you think the throgs control them? They might just be scavengers," Rathe searched for an analogy, "like jackals following the tiger."

"No! The Une-Makhar are on the move. Bands of their warriors roam the north woods, which they claim as their own. Had you continued your journey, Rathe, you would surely have met them. And sometimes Tse'Mara land among their war-parties. I have seen Une-Makhar warriors speak to a Tse'Mara, as a man does to a dog. And —" she paused. "I have heard their tale from their own lips."

"What do you mean?" Rathe asked. He felt a sudden chill. There was something in her tone...

"Ah, but it was at Gothmeg village, you see. I went there, afterwards, to warn them, to rouse their warriors. Silly of me, Rathe. Gothmeg is closer to the throg lands. Of course the Une-Makhar and the Tse'Mara had already come and gone. But I found two throgs who had stayed to loot the dead." She walked over to the pile of skulls, lifted one from the bottom of the heap, caressed it. "He was my first. He told me as much as he could, aye, and he wished to tell me more. For his life ended when his words did."

Orvig worked patiently with the bag, his stubby fingers deftly teasing at the tightly-knotted leather thongs. Finally he had it open. Its contents spilled into his hands.

They were not stones, but rather two dozen disks of bone, each carved with a spidery rune. Even in the dim light of the hut, Orvig recognized them: this was a complete set of the Ithark, the runes of lore, shared by both human and dwarf magickers. While they could not breach the future's veil, it was said that the wise could use them to reveal past and present.

Orvig knew it took power to carve the Ithark, and to make the death-runes he had seen on the spear. Nor would such objects be left unguarded. He stood in a magicker's lair — could this be the seat of his enemy, the one who had caused Jhen to be lost? He thought of a bloody rune drawn on a hard insect shell, and drew his shortsword. The rasp of the blade was answered by a soft hiss.

"I hunt them now," said Kel, her words soft, but sharp as a blade. She had returned the skull to the pile. "It's a strange sensation, Rathe, stalking by daylight rather than night, for the throgs and their beasts prefer the dark and the deep and are drowsy under the sun. Not like hunting animals. But eleven warriors have I sent to join their god. Two have lived long enough to question." Her fingers stroked her sheathed knife. "But I learned little enough. I don't know their tongue, and they knew little of human speech. Perhaps the next one will be different."

Rathe felt repelled by her vindictiveness. Yet in his mind he could see the broken bodies of Dren, Hoth and Nam, and the mangled corpses of the Seth party. *The forest is cruel,* he told himself. What if Orvig or Tam had fallen? Would he make a shrine to vengeance, heaping the skulls of his foes?

Is that why I'm here? The thought disturbed him. *I'm after Jhen,* he told himself. *And answers.*

"Have you heard of a dwarf woman? Maybe hiding from the throgs? Or taken by them?"

"What?" Kelandra tore her gaze away from the grinning trophies. "Oh, your dwarf's sister. Not I. When I came upon your folk on the hill, they had been dead some hours. I heard you speaking of her, that's all. What be her name, Rathe?"

"Jhen Stone—"

Rathe's words were cut short by a sudden yell.

"Help!"

"It's Orvig!" Rathe exclaimed, leaping to his feet. He drew his sword and ran toward the noise. The girl followed on his heels.

The shouting was coming from a small hut at the eastern edge of the village. Rathe thrust its curtain open... and stopped dead.

Orvig was backed into the hut's far corner, a wooden stool held in one hand as a shield, his sword in the other. In front of him swayed a large serpent, easily twice his height, though its body was no wider than his fist.

The mottled snake darted in and out, gliding away from Orvig's sword thrusts with frightening ease. It seemed to be playing with him. The dwarf was breathing in short rasps.

"Rathe," Orvig gasped. "Snake."

"Stay put," Rathe said. He stepped forward, slipping the shield off his back. The snake slid back, turned to meet him, its yellow eyes gleaming in the hut's gloom.

Rathe was ready. He intended to block the snake with the shield and slice off its head with a single blow. If that failed, they could pin it between them. He raised his shield high — and felt Kel's hand on his shoulder.

"Stop! Don't kill him!" Kelandra said. She squeezed past him, and waggled a finger at the snake: "Stupid — can't you tell a dwarf from a throg?"

As Rathe and Orvig looked on, the snake cocked its head and hissed at her, then moved slowly forward. Kel knelt, letting it wrap itself around her arm, its tongue licking delicately at her face.

"He is Akeshi," Kelandra said. She turned to face Rathe. "The keeper of my spirit."

Chapter Four

The snake cradled in her arms, Kelandra surveyed the wreckage of her hut. Broken pots and other debris lay strewn about, scattered by the fight. She shook her head ruefully. "I'll clean this up. Then we can share a meal, if you've a mind."

"That would be welcome," Rathe said. "We can help clean up. Or would you rather we made a cook fire?"

"No!" exclaimed Kel. "Make no blaze in Adra! The Une-Makkar think the village empty now. I'll not change that."

"Fire draws them, then?" Orvig asked.

"Like other beasts, the Tse'Mara fear it," Kel said. "But there may be throgs about. If they see a fire..."

"Fine," said the dwarf. "We'll be outside, if you need us."

He shooed Rathe out, then followed him.

Behind the hut, Rathe confronted the dwarf.

"What's that about?" Rathe demanded. "You were rude. We should have helped her."

"Aye, but I had reason. We need to talk. Let's get away from her hut." Orvig walked a few paces away. Rathe grumbled but followed him. They seated themselves in the long shadow of a tree.

For a long moment, they stared westward. The sun was low in the sky. The forest was quiet, the only sounds the distant cries of nightbirds. Rathe found himself wondering how Tam was doing. Were they nearing Stonekeep? Or had they met the Tse'Mara — or worse?

Orvig broke into his reverie. "Kelandra," he said. He glanced back at the hut. "What do you really know about her, anyway? Why is the village empty? The death-masks?"

"She told me what happened here." Rathe said. He stopped, uncertain how to explain Kel. It was an unusual feeling. He didn't want to hide things from Orvig, but...

"Go on."

"The Whispering Death wiped out the whole village. Kel was the only survivor — she'd been off in the woods when it happened, gathering herbs or something. When she came back, she said the village had been looted — but by throgs. They were controlling the monsters." He paused. "It happened about a month ago. She buried her folk, made the death masks. She's been living here alone ever since."

"Huh," said Orvig. "throgs, eh? So that's what she meant." He tugged angrily at his beard. "And you believe her?"

"Oh yes," said Rathe. *A pile of bleached white bone. I wish I didn't believe her, but I do.* "Look, I know her snake — Akeshi? — gave you a fright, but it doesn't mean she'll do us any harm. It was only protecting her house. You probably frightened it when you were going through her things."

"I don't dispute that, boy. But did you see what I found?"

"No, I was too busy saving you." Rathe chuckled. "You looked ridiculous, waving that stool about. So, what did you find?"

"Magick," Orvig said gravely. "Scrying bones. A rune magick. Did she tell you she was a magicker, boy?"

Rathe remembered the rune-carved staff, planted like a sentinel in front of the skulls. It made sense. "Well, not in so many words. But..."

"And something else, boy. Runes on a spear. Death spells, boy.

We're searching for a shaman who could control the Tse'Mara, boy. Perhaps we've found her, eh?"

"It's not Kel." said Rathe. "I'm certain."

"She's a pretty face, to be sure, but..."

"It's not that!" Rathe said heatedly.

"Oh, aye?" Orvig said innocently.

"I mean, she has good reason. She's the only one left here." He went on, retelling the story of Kel's hunt. The dwarf listened silently, though his eyes narrowed as Rathe spoke of the pile of skulls.

"So she's been stalking the throgs," Rathe finished. "The way she talked about them — I'm sure she wasn't acting. She hates them. So they'd be who the death magick is meant for."

"Hunting them like animals," Orvig said. "And collecting trophies." He looked troubled. "Vengeance can eat your soul."

"Orvig, she came and warned us. We'd have been wiped out if not for her. And she's all that's left of Adra," Rathe said. He shook his head. "Perhaps I'd seek revenge, if my folk were slain by throgs."

"Perhaps," the dwarf echoed. "But throgs controlling those beasts? *That* bothers me. They're warlike, but this kind of massacre — it's not typical for them. And you saw the runes — that's not magick for a normal throg shaman. Think. How many powerful magickers do we know?"

"It's not Kel," Rathe insisted.

"She's making supper, is she? You trust her cooking, boy?"

"Ask her, then," Rathe said, suddenly tiring of his friend's suspicions. Kel had saved their lives — why should she poison them? "If you think it's her, just go ahead and ask her."

"I'd rather eat," Orvig said. He sniffed the air. "I smell food. I think supper's on." He clapped Rathe on the shoulder. "You'd better be right, boy."

They ate outside the hut, on a thick-woven blanket that Kel had brought. It was still light out, although the sun was not long for the sky, and a cool breeze was blowing in from the east.

Kelandra served raw fish garnished with sliced vegetables and covered with a thick, pungent sauce. Rathe found the prospect less than appetizing, but it was a change from trail rations, and it tasted better than it smelled. Afterwards, he complimented Kel on her meal.

"I'm used to cooking without fire," Kel explained. "I catch the fish in a stream a mile from here. Sometimes Akeshi and I hunt together."

Orvig's gaze strayed back to the door of the hut.

Kel grinned nastily. "He frightened you! I forgot. But I left him sleeping. Don't worry. He won't harm you now."

"And you, lady?" said Orvig easily.

"You're no throg." She turned to face him, eyes hard. "Their Tse'Mara pets slew your sister, not so? Your enemy is mine, dwarf."

Rathe winced.

"Maybe," said Orvig. "Yet I am not ready to make a pile of skulls." He paused. "Besides, Jhen may live."

"How so?" said Kel coldly, not looking up. She speared a fresh chunk of fish with her knife. "In their killing rage, the Tse'Mara take no prisoners. They leave only death."

"Blood," Orvig said. "Rathe said he spoke of the rune to you. It drives them to kill, does it not?"

"That's truth," muttered Kel, through a mouthful of fish. "The blood-rune binds them to hate the smell of human blood, so — oh!"

She met Orvig's gaze. "You could be right."

"Yes, maybe not dwarf blood." Orvig nodded. "So Rathe and I guessed."

"Could they have taken her?" Rathe asked.

"It's possible," Kel admitted. "They took no prisoners here, nor at Gothmeg. But I really don't know."

"You told Rathe you were watching Seth's caravan," Orvig said. "Did you... " He stopped.

Kel's snake had left the hut and slithered toward them.

Kel darted a glance at Orvig. She smiled slightly, then scooped the snake into her arms. "Be still, Akeshi," she said. "You were saying?"

"Thank you," said Orvig. "You saw no sign of Jhen?"

"No," she said. "I did not see the battle. I'd been hunting near

Gothmeg when I came upon tracks leading northeast. I read the signs, and guessed they were made by two or three dozen throgs and perhaps a score of Tse'Mara."

"Did you see where they went?"

"I followed them for the rest of the day. But that night, I saw wings against the moon. A dozen Tse'Mara had turned back south." She shrugged. "I made a choice. I'd gone far from Adra already. And I wanted to see what they were hunting, so I turned back also." She looked at Rathe.

"You hadn't found the massacre yet?" Rathe asked.

"No. But the rains came then, and the Tse'Mara went to ground. They don't like to fly in wet weather. It was then that I found the slaughter-ground and saw you two and the warrior-girl atop the hill. I listened to your speech, and when you spoke of the weapons and loot being gone, I knew it was your folk the Tse'Mara and throgs had slain, ere they went north. But for some reason they were back. I guessed they'd come to hunt you."

The girl shuddered as she remembered. "Yes, the Whispering Death were watching you, Rathe, though you didn't see them. They were there in the wood as you buried your dead. They stalked your warband as you marched southward and made camp. After the rain stopped and night fell, I knew they would attack before dawn. So I warned you." She reached out and, to Rathe's surprise, traced the scar on his forehead. "But I was almost too late."

"It was well for us that you did," Rathe said. He frowned as a thought struck him. "But you're saying the throgs were moving north, and then suddenly they decided to send their creatures back south — almost as if they received word that we were coming."

"It's odd," said Kel. "I hadn't thought of that part. But I saw no scouts..."

"Magick," interjected Orvig suddenly. "Whoever controlled the creatures was warned of our coming. By magick."

"To see across the miles?" said Kel. She stared into space, absently stroking her familiar. "It would take a powerful magick."

"The runes of Ithark, lady?" said Orvig. "Would they have the power?"

The snake hissed. "So you know," Kel said coldly. "You took time to search my hut, then?"

"And recognized the rune-spear and the Ithark bones." admitted Orvig. "Strong runes, Kelandra of Adra. Deadly runes. How came you by them?"

The truce is over, Rathe thought.

Kel's green eyes flashed and she leaned forward, staring directly at Orvig. "I owe no answer to you, dwarf!" she said. "Yes, I am rune-wise. I could have — " she paused. "I was to be my people's shaman." She narrowed her eyes. "Nor am I the only one here with magick. What of the talisman Rathe bears?"

"My ring?" Rathe said. "You mentioned it earlier. What of it?"

"It seemed familiar," she said. "I'm not sure why." She shrugged. "But I know it is a thing of power. Am I right? Are there runes upon it?"

"Yes," Rathe said. "Fine lines carved in the jewel, hard to see." He paused. "The rune reminded me of something."

"Rathe — " said Orvig warningly.

"The blood–rune on the Tse'Mara?" Kelandra guessed. She studied Rathe's face. "I thought as much."

"How did you know?" Rathe asked.

"You think we had something to do with the beasts?" Orvig demanded.

"If it's true, I'd have reason, would I not?" she said. She glared at Orvig. "Greater reason than you had to accuse me." She squatted down next to Rathe. "But I don't. May I?"

Kelandra took his wrist in her hands, holding it up to the light, studying the ring's black depths without touching it. "Cats! You're right, it's too dark to read the finer marks. We'll have to wait until morning." She glared at the setting sun. "Khull-Khuum, never there when you need him, always there when you don't."

"Hold hard," Rathe said. "I just remembered." He got up, and looked around for his pack, found it just inside the hut. He opened it and removed the pen-and-ink sketch he had made for Orvig. He passed it over to Kel.

She unfolded it gingerly, then stared.

"Wandering Gods!" she exclaimed. "I thought so. It's kin to the blood rune on the Tse'Mara, all right. But that rune is only a part, the merest shadow of the whole." Her fingers shook as she traced the symbols. "These lines here — power, great power. And those, they have to do with preservation or healing. "But this section here is obliterated — what it meant, I cannot tell." She looked at Rathe. "Is your ring flawed?"

"Flawed? No," Rathe said. He held up his finger. "You can see the stone is unmarred. I drew this before I saw the ring."

Kel cocked her head. "Before? I'd like to hear that tale."

"During the battle, one of the creatures struck me, and I fell. I slept . . . my comrades thought I was dying. But I dreamed of a strange chamber, and a woman's voice, speaking to me."

Kel listened attentively as Rathe related what the voice had told him, and his "escape" from the dream. He went on to describe how they had discovered the Tse'Mara's rune, and what Orvig had revealed to him about his parentage.

"So you see, until recently, I did not know of my legacy," Rathe said. He glanced at Orvig sharply.

"I had my reasons," Orvig said wearily. "They seemed good to me then."

"So your mother was a priestess of Thera," whispered Kel. Her voice was shaky. "And she left you when you were a child. What was her name, Rathe?"

"Rhea," Rathe said. "Kel, what's the matter?"

"Gods," said Kel. She shook her head. "That would explain much."

"What do you mean?" said Orvig.

Kel started, as if she hadn't realized she'd been speaking aloud. She paused for a few seconds as if gathering her thoughts, then began speaking in a stronger, more deliberate tone.

"That was no dream, Rathe. We can be sure of that. It was a sending," Kel said. "I think — I believe — that Thera spoke to you herself."

"The goddess?" Rathe said. "But that can't be." And yet, as he remembered the sheer *presence* of the voice, he wondered. Yet reason held sway. "Save Khull-Khuum, the gods are gone. How could Thera speak to me?"

"You are of the blood of a high priestess, Rathe," answered Kel. "And something calls to that blood. Something — the goddess, maybe — wants you. Has chosen you." She looked at him steadily for a moment. "But what do *you* want, Rathe?"

"To find Jhen," Rathe said. "And to learn who is behind the Tse'Mara." He looked grim. "There are lives between us."

"Then we share a foe." Kelandra turned to Orvig. "You spoke of the Ithark runes, dwarf. Yes, I have their art. I can use them to try and discover what power lay behind the throgs — and to seek your sister."

"If it works, I will be grateful," Orvig said. "But you had the runes. Why didn't you seek your foes before? Haven't you tried before now?"

"I've tried," she admitted. "But this time it should work."

"Why did you fail before?" said Orvig. "Do you lack skill?"

"No!" she exclaimed angrily. Startled, the snake wriggled in her grip, and she patted its head. "Say rather that something blocked my vision. There is a — " she struggled for a word " — a veil I could not pierce. Their shaman — or whatever he is — is powerful."

"If there's a chance of finding Jhen, we should take it," Rathe said. "But why *do* you think it will work now, Kel?"

Kel's emerald eyes met his own.

"Because of you, Rathe."

An hour later, Rathe stood by the village well, dripping wet and shivering slightly. At Kel's urging, he'd bathed — "to purify the body," she'd said. As he dressed, he thought about what Kel had told him: as the son of a priestess, his blood had power.

It had been a long day, but Rathe didn't feel tired — in fact, he was exhilarated. He probed his feelings, and realized what it was. Something was about to happen.

He would aid her in the ritual.

Back in the hut, Kel and Orvig made their preparations, now

reluctant allies.

"The sun's about to set," Orvig said.

"Better," said Kel. "I'd rather not do this under Khull-Khuum's eye, anyway. The throgs worship him as their chief god."

"Odd," said Orvig "since they hide from his rays."

"Think like a throg," Kel said. "They respect power. And worship what they fear. But anyway, we'll need to make a light." She found a candle. "My uncle had one of your fire-makers, but the Une-Makkar took it. Have you flint and steel?"

"Aye," said Orvig. He opened his bulging pack, rummaged noisily through it.

"What have you got in there?" Kel asked. She leaned over, curious, and peered inside. Bottles, metal implements... she shook her head.

"Tools of the trade," Orvig grunted. "Never know when you might need something. Here we go. Better than rubbing two sticks together." He hesitated and eyed the circle that Kel had carved in the dirt floor of her hut. "Will this really work, lass?"

Kel nodded. She had drawn it with her spear and made five runes. Three of them Orvig recognized as protective. Two were unfamiliar. Kel had told them they were spirit-anchors.

"Is it dangerous?" Orvig said.

"For Rathe?" She considered. "I don't think so. Now, where did I put that oil?"

When Rathe returned, a faint light spilled from Kel's hut: a single beeswax candle, casting a lambent glow. Rathe opened the door flap and entered. Kel turned to face him — and he caught his breath.

Kelandra had discarded her skin garments for the black feather cloak. Through its folds, her slim body shone as if oiled, reflecting the candlelight. Her dark hair, freshly combed, fell down to her shoulders in a single wave. Akeshi, the snake, was curled about her waist, a dark living belt. She was beautiful, Rathe realized. But more than that, she radiated power — an aura he could actually feel. She held a doeskin bag and her rune-carved spear.

Rathe did not doubt that she was a shaman.

"Are you ready, Rathe?" Kel said. Her green eyes burned with a curious intensity.

"I am," he said, throat dry. "What do I do?"

"Orvig said you know the tune called `Hinternight?'"

"Yes," said Rathe, surprised. "It's a Stonekeep trail song."

"It's older than that," Kelandra said. "Start by humming it. Here," she said. "You'll need this." She handed him the bag. Rathe took it, and opened the string. It held small disks of carved bone.

"The Ithark runes?" he asked.

"Place your hand in the bag," Kel said, "and feel them. Rub them together."

Rathe did as he was told. They were cool to the touch, their thin edges worn smooth with time.

"Watch me. When you feel the time is right, draw the disk that feels right, and cast it into the circle, and I will follow its path to what is and what was. Then I will speak, and you must listen. Say nothing, but listen carefully — I may not remember what I said."

"What about Orvig?"

"I know what to do," he said gruffly. "You just find Jhen."

With Kelandra crouched beside him, Orvig began to hum the old song, Rathe following his lead, its familiar tune carrying him along.

As they hummed, Kel began a strange dance, slow and sinuous, moving with the rhythmic tune, light and shadow playing upon her body as the feather cloak swirled about her. Akeshi had slid down from her waist, the snake's pattern interweaving with hers.

The sing-song humming and Kel's serpentine motion were hypnotic. As she danced, Rathe felt the disks of bone sliding between his fingers as if following the patterns she made. And suddenly, Rathe realized her dance was a rune, an ever-changing symbol, drawn and redrawn in the movements of her body.

His fingers knew which rune it was. They acted.

The bone disk fell at her feet before he realized he had tossed it. Like a puppet, Kelandra jerked, twisted, her body contorting to follow the jagged pattern of the rune. She ended frozen in a half crouch, arms akimbo, eyes closed.

And began to speak.

"The rune Jechandra calls me to the path," Kel said. Her voice was distant. Rathe leaned closer to hear.

"The path of blood and dreams. But not alone."

Kel's voice changed, grew older. She opened her eyes and stared right at him. "I speak to you, rune-master. A power moves you, stirs in your blood and your dreams. That which is broken must be repaired. You tread the road of gods and kings. But it is a great journey, and yours is but the first step. A finger cannot move mountains, but a single pebble can unleash the avalanche. Now something rises in your path. It has been awakened, discovered. Not by chance, no. By design. A third force. Hidden by illusions, veiled in lies, amused by death..."

Rathe shivered. It wasn't Kel's voice. What did it mean?

"Gone," said Kel. It was her own voice, but somehow muted, far away. "She is gone, now. But my eyes have been opened and I know where to look."

"I see the deep places of the Shadow's Teeth. The throg warriors are chanting to the beat of drums. I see the mad dancing of the Tse'Mara, chained by runes of blood. I see the dungeons, dark and wet, and the lost soul trapped within."

Her voice grew louder and wilder.

"I see the shaman in his feathered cloak, stained with the blood of eagles. His eyes are old and mad. He holds something else in his hand, cold as ice, black as night, sharp as glass. Something stolen. Something broken, lost and mad. It has eyes. They open..."

"And they see me." said Kel. "They see me. Oh, they see me! Akeshi! Stop him. Something's coming! I hear it buzzing."

The snake hissed and uncoiled, rearing up as if to strike. Its head wove back and forth, as if tracking an invisible foe. It seemed to focus on something. Then, suddenly, the graceful body froze, slumped to the ground. The snake's head struck with a soft thump, sending up a little cloud of dust.

"No!" Kel screamed. "Akeshi, where are you?"

Rathe didn't know what to do. What was happening? Kel had

said not to act, but something was wrong. But what could he do? Was Kel trapped in a nightmare? Should he try to wake her?

"I can hear them!" Kel exclaimed. She looked wildly about. "Where are they? Buzzing, buzzing! They're coming!"

Something was wrong!

"Kel, there's nothing here!" Rathe said desperately.

"Stay out of the circle," Orvig warned. "It's not safe."

"No!" said Rathe. "She's in danger." He stepped forward. He took Kel in his arms, shook her. "Kel, wake up!"

"But can't you see them? Insects! They're in my hair!" She began slapping at her body, scratching and clawing at her hair.

"Kel!" Rathe shouted. He ran his hand through her dark tresses. There was nothing there. "It's just a dream! Come back!"

"Keep back, boy," said Orvig. "She's having a fit." He stepped forward, slapped her face. "Snap out of it, girl!"

"No!" she screamed. She struggled wildly, tearing at her skin, her nails leaving long red marks in the tanned flesh. "Get them off!" With surprising strength, she broke free, spinning away from Rathe, knocking Orvig to the ground. The dwarf staggered back, tripped over a stool. He bounced off the wall and slumped to the ground, stunned. Kel didn't even notice. She staggered back. "It's him! He sent them! Oh, Gods, inside me! They're eating me alive!"

It wasn't just a fit, Rathe realized. The other shaman! The foe had torn through Kel's defenses, her veil. But how could he save her? He held his sword, but there was nothing to cut.

But what could he do? He stared at his useless hands. The ring, mark of a priestess, mocked him.

A tortured moan was torn from Kel's throat. Beyond words, she had doubled over and dropped to all fours. Her belly heaved, mouth open as if to retch. But nothing came out. Her face was twisted in anguish.

Someone was killing her! Thera help him, he had to act! He focused his desire, imagined the rune in his dream, the complete rune that he had seen before it shattered.

He saw it as a black glass lens that would show him the truth. He willed himself to *see* what was hurting her, to pierce the veil, to perceive what Kel saw — and suddenly, he could.

A half-dozen palm-sized insects swarmed over Kelandra's body. Cruel clawed legs dug into her flesh. Jaws bit, tearing and gouging. The creatures were like tiny Tse'Mara — and yet unlike them, for these were solid black, living chunks of darkness without detail, save for a single spot of color. And the wounds they opened in her body closed seconds later of their own accord!

And yet, they hurt her — Kel writhed in agony. The creatures might not be able to do lasting harm, but the pain was real, and Rathe feared what injury they were doing to her mind and soul.

As he stared, horror-stricken, Kel clutched her throat and gagged. Her mouth opened wide. A spiky head emerged from her gaping mouth, followed by barbed legs. It pulled its way out. Like the others, it had a blood-red rune glowing on its belly.

The blood–rune! The same as on the Tse'Mara. Kel had called it a shadow, a perversion. But on his finger was the real rune. What if light met darkness? Rathe made a fist, touched his ring finger to the creature in her mouth — and it melted into black smoke.

The other creatures drew back, halted their attacks. Black antennae swivelled. Invisible eyes stared at Rathe. Wings spread, a challenge — or a preparation to attack?

But Rathe held up the ring, focused on it. His first success had given him confidence. "You are nothing," he told them. He forced a smile. "Shadows without substance. Reflections in a broken mirror." He shook his head. "Less than nothing. Begone!"

And the creatures melted into darkness.

The battle was over. In the corner, Orvig groaned, rubbing his bruised head. The snake, Akeshi, lay still and lifeless.

Rathe knelt in the dirt circle, holding Kelandra cradled in his arms. He called her name, over and over.

Suddenly her eyes flew open.

"Akeshi," she said. "He's dead."

"I know," Rathe said, remembering the snake's actions. "He tried to save you."

Her shoulders shook. Rathe realized she was crying. He hugged her, holding her tightly until the sobs subsided.

She turned to face him, wiped away a tear, eyes red. "I don't — it's just, after Adra — " she paused. "When everyone else was gone, he was the only one."

"You're not alone now," Rath e said. Gently, he stroked her hair. "Not any more."

"Yes," Kel agreed. One arm went around him.

Rathe felt her body relax.

In a moment, she was asleep.

Chapter Five

Orvig was shaking him. "Rathe! Wake up, boy."

Rathe blinked sleep out of his eyes. The hut's door was open. The faint light of early morning spilled through.

He looked around. There was no sign of Kel. "Where is she?" Rathe asked. He sat up.

"Outside by the forest. She's laying her snake to rest. She said she wanted to be alone."

"Did she look all right?" Rathe worried. "She could be in trouble."

"She *is* trouble!" Orvig said. He touched his forehead, winced. There was a bright purple bruise there. "She seemed in good shape. But something happened last night, boy. She began speaking. Or something spoke through her. Then what? Her spell went wrong?"

"I don't know, exactly." said Rathe. He pulled his clothes on absently, thinking back. "The throg shaman — I think he sensed her. He struck back, somehow killed Akeshi. The snake was her familiar, trying to protect her. Then he went after her. But we got her out of it."

"We? My head may have been ringing like a master's anvil. But I know I didn't do anything."

Rathe nodded. "It's hard to believe. It was killing her — an illusion, maybe. I don't know. I concentrated on the rune, the one in my dream, and I was able to see them." Rathe grimaced.

"Aye," said Orvig. "Shadows, you said."

"Shadows of the Tse'Mara," Rathe answered. "They bore the same rune as the real thing. I remembered what Kel had said, and thought the whole rune might have power over them." He smiled grimly. "It did."

"You commanded them to vanish?" Orvig said. "And they did." He shook his head. "I saw you. It was strange — or maybe not so strange. You had her look..."

"What do you mean?" Rathe said.

Orvig didn't speak for a long moment. "I saw it on your mother's face once. When she was healing a boy who was near death. He was at the brink. She wouldn't give up. And she brought him back." The dwarf looked sober.

"Was my mother a rune-mage?" Rathe said.

"She was, boy." Orvig looked sober. "I think you are, too."

Smoke swirled skyward from the crackling pyre by the forest's edge. There was a smell of burning meat and incense. Kel was there, dressed in her skins, but wearing her feather cloak.

"I make no mask for Akeshi," said Kel. She turned to Rathe. Her eyes were dry. "His spirit goes to the winds."

"To the winds," Rathe repeated. He rested his hand on her shoulder. "I'm sorry, Kel."

She shrugged him off. "We have to go," Kel said. She had a bundled pack at her feet. "I can't stay here."

"Especially since that fire said 'here we are' to every throg and insect within a dozen miles," grumbled Orvig. "Couldn't you just bury him?"

"Orvig," warned Rathe.

But Kel didn't take offense.

"He's a snake, not a man," she said, still watching the drifting plume. "He has no mask. It's the way. The fire doesn't matter, anyway."

"What do you mean?" Orvig said.

"Rathe should know," Kel said.

Rathe considered — "Gods!" he exclaimed. "The shaman — does he know we're here?"

"Yes," Kel said. "That's how he attacked me. I'm sorry, I should have told you." She plucked a twig from a tree, snapped it. "I just..."

"You weren't in any shape," said Rathe. "None of us were."

It was true. The battle had left him exhausted.

"So we move out." Orvig sighed, staring at the tiny funeral pyre. "Where? We still don't know where to find Jhen."

"But we do," Kel said. "I saw your sister."

"What?" said Orvig.

"The lost soul..." said Rathe. "That was Jhen?"

"Yes," said Kel. "She seemed unharmed."

"Unharmed!" A grin spread over Orvig's face. He reached up and hugged her. "Kelandra of Adra, I thank you."

"It was hard won," Kel said. She squeezed free. Then her face softened, melted by Orvig's joy. "She looked so young!"

"We grow slowly," said Orvig lightly. He stepped back. "She's older than you, I'd guess." He took Kel's hand. "Tell me! What else?"

"Oh. She's underground. A small chamber, rough hewn. Water drips from the ceiling. She was counting the drops. There was someone with her. A throg, I think. He was very old. They were speaking."

"What did they say?" Rathe asked. *Jhen was alive!*

"I don't know. They spoke in the throg tongue. A light burned just outside. A lamp. It hurt the throg's eyes. That's all."

"Jhen knows the throg language?"

"She's good at things like that." Orvig said. "She's a trader."

"Jhen wasn't all you saw," Rathe said. He didn't want to press her, but... "You spoke of the Shadow's Teeth."

"We know that name," Orvig said. "The foothills by the broken lands, where the forest ends." He looked at Rathe. "Do you still have Hoth's map?"

"It's back in the hut," he said. "Is that where she is?"

"I think so," Kel said. She was still holding the twig. Now she knelt and began scratching in the ground. "Here we are, at Adra," she pointed. She picked up a pebble, eyed the sun, then plunked it down. "Gothmeg," she decided, "a day north." She drew a line running north and east. "The Shadow's Teeth."

"But where in the Teeth?" Rathe asked.

Kel's face fell. "I don't know."

"You also spoke of the Shaman," Orvig said. "What of him?"

"Don't press her," Rathe said. "That was when the attack..."

"No," she said. "It's all right. He was a throg," Kel said slowly. "Younger than the one with Jhen. His face was cruel. He wore a feathered cloak, like mine. But his was stained with blood." She hugged herself. "He had something with him, like a skull, but carved from black glass — its eyes —" Kel began to shake. She turned to Rathe, her own eyes wide. "They opened. They saw! Oh, Gods!"

"It's all right," Rathe said. "You're back. It's over."

She took a deep breath, gathered her thoughts. "It looked like a human skull. And on its forehead was a rune. The rune that was carved on the Tse'Mara."

"This skull — what was it?" Rathe asked. "A talisman?"

"An object of power," Kel agreed. "But it was also alive, Rathe. And — I'm not sure, but I think it was in pain."

"It was made of glass?" Orvig asked.

"Volcanic glass," Kel said. "Obsidian, like Rathe's ring."

"And like the temple in my dream!" Rathe exclaimed.

They left the village quickly. "Adra is dead," she told Rathe. "There's nothing left for me here."

Kel led them north, by the secret paths her people had known. The day was cooler than it had been, for clouds were gathering in the west. They saw a black bear and two cubs, but no sign of Tse'Mara, man or throg. Once, they heard a beat of wings. Kel shooed them into the bushes, but it was only a large hawk.

"Next time, don't pick a thorn bush," Orvig said. "Ouch."

"I've some salve," said Kel. She pulled a small clay pot from her pack. "Here, let me."

"I thought the Tse'Mara hunt only by night?" Rathe asked.

"They do," she answered "but it is by choice, not law. Their eyes are poorer, and the light bothers them. But I think this shaman could drive them to hunt by day, if his will was strong enough." She shrugged, then raised an eyebrow at Orvig. "Better scratched than dead."

When night came, Kel said they were some miles east of Gothmeg, Adra's sister village.

"How much farther?" Orvig asked.

"We must find a river, the Erderli," she told them. "It runs cold and swift. I think we'll reach it around noon next day, if we keep up this pace. When we reach it, we follow its bank for half a day, then turn east."

"We've made good time," Rathe said.

"Yes," Kel agreed. "Tomorrow we'll see mountains."

Kel drew the first watch, Rathe the last. It was a few hours before dawn. The night was cloudless and bright with stars, but a chill wind whistled among the hills.

His watch wore on. Orvig lay sleeping like a log, his breathing slow and steady. But Kel's blanket had slipped off, and she stirred fretfully, murmuring, as the wind whipped through her hair. He bent to listen, fearful that something was wrong, that the fit had returned. But it was only names she was speaking: Akeshi, other names — relatives, lovers?

Did she walk with them in pleasant memories, when they still lived? Or was it a nightmare? He hesitated, reluctant to wake her. Then, afraid she would catch a chill, Rathe drew the blanket back over her. He reached out and touched her cheek. She stirred slightly, then seemed to settle down.

Both of them had lost their parents, Rathe realized. They shared that bleak bond. He held up his hand to the starlight, stared at the ring on his finger. Kel had her memories, however painful, while he could only summon vague images. His mother's scent, a snatch of cradlesong, a toy he had played with.

But he still had Orvig. He gazed at the sleeping dwarf. He wished Orvig had told him about his parents' fate before. And yet, he could not get angry. He cared too much for the old dwarf. To his heart, Orvig was his father, too. He would find Jhen, he vowed. Orvig's family was his own.

Dawn came, and with it a thick mist.

"I doubt we'll see mountains in this soup," Rathe told Kelandra over breakfast. "Or be able to find our way."

"It will slow us, but it will also hide us from prying eyes." Kel answered. "We need only find the river."

"If we don't lose our way and fall in quicksand instead," grumbled Orvig.

"Trust me," Kel said.

They marched in silence, the enveloping fog stifling conversation, muffling all sounds, even their footsteps. Soon the ground was no longer flat, but undulated in a series of low hills. They moved slowly but steadily, Kel apparently unafraid of becoming lost. She held her spear out, occasionally stopping for a second, moving it back and forth, much as a blind man would use a walking stick. It was odd.

Rathe decided to try something. He imagined the rune — Thera's rune — and concentrated, willing himself to *see*, in the same way he had seen the shadow-beasts.

A warm amber glow was coming from the spear, from the third rune along its shaft. As Kel moved the spear back and forth, it changed in intensity, the glow increasing as she pointed it to the left. Kel nodded to herself, and led them off in that direction.

Aha, Rathe thought. *I was right.*

It was noon when they heard the sound of running water. They had reached the Erderli, as it wound its way north.

"You're a trusty guide," Rathe said.

"It wasn't going anywhere," Kel replied, but she smiled at him, glad of the praise.

It was mid-afternoon, and they were resting ere they continued on through evening. Orvig and Kel had gone to refill the canteens by the river. Rathe could see Orvig, although Kel had vanished. He frowned — they'd both promised to stay within earshot.

Rathe sat in the shadow of a tree. Hoth's map was spread out before him, and he was marking the route they had traveled as best he could, filling in the white space. The sun was warm on his back. The forest might be full of foes, and he kept his sword beside him. But for now, at least, it seemed peaceful.

The sun had burned away the mist, and the river lay before them, its west bank overgrown with willow and sycamore. A trill of birdsong mixed with the chirp of crickets. The day had turned warm, and the sun sent bright shafts through the forest canopy.

When he heard the rustle above him, he reached for his blade. A musical laugh drifted down. He looked up.

Kel was perched on the oak's limb, long legs swinging.

"Hey, Rathe — can you catch me?" she said.

"Kel!" Rathe exclaimed.

She laughed again, and then hooked her legs about the branch, and swung, upside down, her hair dangling down. "Keep-folk can't climb," she taunted, her voice a sing-song.

That was it. With a mock growl, Rathe scrambled after her. Laughing, she fled, agile as a monkey. He caught her halfway up, but somehow he was sure she let him. Kel teetered, nearly falling, and he put his arm about her waist to steady her.

She turned her head and kissed him.

"Kel..."

"For saving my life," she said.

"May I?" Rathe asked. She looked into his eyes, green as her own, and nodded twice. They kissed again. It lasted a long time before they broke apart.

They sat in silence, watching the rushing river below them. But their eyes were drawn northward, where the hills grew greater in the distance, until they merged as one with the sky.

"The Shadow's Teeth," Rathe said.

"We'll reach them tomorrow," Kel agreed. "When we get there, what will you do?"

"Find Jhen," said Rathe. "Yourself?"

"I still have a debt to pay."

"And afterwards?"

She shook her head, then looked down. "Oh, cats," Kel said. Rathe followed her gaze.

Orvig was standing below, holding a string of water bottles. He shook his finger at her.

"Oops," said Kel. "I forgot to help fill the bottles."

Orvig and Rathe went to wash their clothes in the river. Rathe had cleaned his back at Adra, so he finished first. When he returned, he saw Kel bent over his map. She looked up, guiltily.

"Sorry," Kel said. She put it down.

"It's all right," Rathe replied. "It's not a secret." He handed it back to her.

She ran her fingers over the parchment, looking at the region near Stonekeep. "It's so detailed," she said wonderingly. "Did you draw it yourself?"

"No," said Rathe. "It was made by Wren, a master cartographer, back at Stonekeep. Do you understand it?"

"Not really," said Kel. "I'm not sure what the symbols mean."

"They're like runes," said Rathe. "But not magical. Here, let me show you how to read it."

He described the map, and showed Kel what the marks for distance meant. "Here we are," he said. He traced a path through white space. "The Shadow's Teeth."

"That line," Kel pointed. "The Erderli river, yes?"

Rathe nodded.

"But why does it stop before Gothmeg?" She stabbed down with her finger. "We're over here."

"Because our map-makers hadn't been this far," Rathe laughed. "Truth to tell, we're not even sure exactly where the mountains are. When I get back to Stonekeep, they'll make a new map — I'll have to help draw it." He grinned. "But until then, we rely on your talents. You used magick, didn't you? In the fog?"

"Yes," said Kel admitted. "A rune of direction. But how did you know? Or did you guess?"

"It's hard to explain." He hesitated. "I focused on the rune, Thera's rune. And willed myself to see. There was a warm glow when you used the spear — you followed it? Is that what you saw?"

Kel shook her head. "Magick is different for everyone. I felt a kind of tug, not a glow. But yes. The spear guided me."

"Orvig said your spear held death runes," Rathe said, speaking in a low voice. "It doesn't, does it?"

"He's no rune master," Kel replied. "A rune has many faces, Rathe." She stared out into the river. "Felmurg, the rune that guided us through the fog, also holds the spear true when I throw it into a foe's heart." She put her hands on her hips, and gave him a quizzical look. "Don't they teach magick at Stonekeep?"

"They do," said Rathe. "But I was never chosen to learn the art."

"The more fools them," she said. "What's it like?"

"The Keep?"

"Yes." She took Rathe's hand in both of hers. "Tell me."

"It's very different from living here, deep in the forest," Rathe said. "And yet the forest is part of all our lives..." Rathe described the huge citadel of the Keep, towering over the forest, its many halls and winding underground passages. Kelandra listened raptly, sometimes shaking her head, but made no comment till Rathe described its thousands of inhabitants.

"That many? But what do they all do?"

"Most of us are loggers, working in the forest."

"Not farmers or hunters?" She was skeptical. "Do you eat wood?"

"No," Rathe grinned. He saw Orvig returning, bearing his laundry, face and beard wet. "We leave that to the Dwarves."

"You're teasing me," Kel said.

"A little," Rathe admitted. "Some of us are hunters, and we gather fruit and nuts in season, same as you. But the Dwarves dwell deep beneath our halls, and grow mushrooms in their caves. In return, we bring them timber to frame their passages and stoke their furnaces. They forge good steel." He slapped his sword.

"So that's why your folk gather wood!" said Kel. She turned to face Orvig. "Are you a mushroom farmer?" Kel asked him, "Or a smith?"

"Neither," replied Orvig, proudly. "My clan is the Stonemelters."

"You melt stone?" Kel asked. "Why?"

"We brew strong acids. To etch rock into carvings," Orvig said. "We also make other goods, like glass, from things like sand. Have you seen a telescope?"

"No," said Kel. "But I've heard of them."

"I wish I had one with me," Orvig said glumly. "Maybe we could spot that mountain."

They shared a meal of dried fish and cheese, then resumed their journey. They scoured the river bank for trails that would take them from the foothills into the mountains. Late in the afternoon, they found one — an old game track. Kel stopped to read the signs: It had been used, and recently. A dozen booted feet. And other prints. It led northeast. They followed it.

Kel walked in front, with Rathe beside her. Their eyes scanned the trail, but they talked easily, speaking of the differences between the trees in this place and those around Stonekeep. Orvig brought up the rear, staying silent, though he smiled sometimes, as if to himself.

Suddenly, Kel froze. "Tse'Mara," she hissed. Quick as a serpent, she vanished behind a boulder. Rathe and Orvig scurried for hiding places. Rathe found himself in the bushes at the base of a small pine. He peered out.

Whispering Death. There was only one, but it still sent shudders down Rathe's spine. A thing of glittering armor and flashing spikes and wings, it was beautiful in its sheer deadly grace. It circled, humming to itself. Was it after them? Rathe's hand closed tightly on the hilt of his sword, and he slowly unfastened the shield from his back.

It furled its wings and dived, stooping like a hawk. Rathe's heart leaped into his mouth, afraid that it had spotted Orvig or Kel. There was a squeal of pain — and then the Death emerged, a small rabbit impaled on its forearm spike. Rathe breathed a sigh of relief. Hunting, but not for them.

The creature launched itself into the air, alighting on a nearby tree. A cloud of pine needles showered down. Perched on it, the Tse'Mara looked like an exotic weathercock. It stared down at its captive, compound eyes reflecting myriad rabbit-images. The agonized creature mewled piteously as it writhed on the spikes. Then the Tse'Mara bent over, and its jaws closed on the rabbit's head. Blood splattered. It slurped up what was left with a wet sucking sound, then dropped the carcass and launched itself skyward, wings buzzing, toward the east. Soon it dwindled to a black dot.

The sun was an orange glow, low in the sky. They were among the foothills now, climbing steadily. The mountains loomed high above them, covered with a dense pine forest. That evening, they found a place to camp, a small copse a score of paces from the summit of a low hill. Their supper was meager — the last of the bread and cheese, two onions, and the remnants of Kel's fish. Their rations were nearly gone. They would last another day, at most.

"We should have taken that rabbit," remarked Rathe. "The one the Death threw away." Orvig looked at him suspiciously, but Kelandra just nodded. "It had no rune. It was just a wild hunter. It was dangerous, but not magic."

"Who takes first watch?" Rathe asked. He was dead tired, but doubted the others felt any better.

"We'll be in poor shape for tomorrow," Orvig grumbled.

"Orvig's right," Kel said. "Tomorrow we reach the mountains. We need some rest." She reached into her pack, and removed a small wicker cage. It held the skeleton of a bird.

"That was in your hut," Orvig said, surprised. "What is it?"

"A talisman," Kel said. "I can use it once, without a lengthy cleansing."

Rathe watched, fascinated, as Kel plucked a feather out of her cloak, pricked her finger with its tip, and then sketched a delicate rune on the bird's skull, over each tiny eye socket. "Sybaris," she said. "The Guardian." She addressed the bird, "Watch well, spirit of the forest. If throg or beast or man approaches, wake us." She hung the cage on the tree limb. "We can rest easily, tonight. But don't leave its sight, or the spell will be broken. If foes come, Sybaris will give warning — but not much."

"Dead tree and dead birds," said Orvig gloomily. He yawned. "I hope this works better than the Ithark."

"If you toss a pebble and your foe replies with a spear, is your aim any less true? The shaman was stronger than I thought." She scowled. "Next time I'll be ready."

Rathe's eyes were drawn back to the wicker cage. He fell asleep wondering what call a dead bird would make. The image haunted his dreams, and he saw skeletal ravens flying over a forest of dark trees whose leaves were broken glass. Then, suddenly, a shadow fell across the forest. The leaves shattered and fell to the ground with a sound like a thousand broken mirrors.

Rathe woke with a jump. He saw Orvig as the dwarf snatched up his sword. He looked up. The dead bird's cage slowly rotated in the tree.

There was no wind.

"Ssssshh!" hissed Kel. "throgs!"

Rathe lay crouched down, face pressed into the brush. Kel was on his left, Orvig behind him. He couldn't see the throgs, but he heard their harsh voices, calling to each other, the snap of twigs as they widened the path through the wood, the clank of metal and the creak of leather. Their croaking language seemed a blending of frog and bird — and yet, he thought, it had a complex, rhythmic structure that spoke of intelligence.

They lay still for some minutes. The band was going north.

Kel and Rathe studied the tracks. "Five of them," Kel said. "A small party. Probably hunters."

"What now?" said Orvig. He yawned. "Back to sleep?"

"No! We need them to lead us to their stronghold," Rathe said. "This may be our only chance." He looked at Kel. She nodded. "We follow them." said Rathe. "And pray we don't run into any Tse'Mara."

They stalked the throgs through the night, following them eastward, over hill and vale. An hour before dawn, they heard a whisper of wings. The throgs were a hundred paces ahead of them.

"Tse'Mara!"

This time it was not just one, though how many they couldn't tell.

Kel urged him to take cover. "I want to see," said Rathe.

"It's too dark," said Kel. "They'll smell you before you see them." She held him back.

Hardly breathing, they listened. The humming rose in intensity, and mingled with the throgs' own voices. Then the creatures rose again. The humming grew in strength — they were heading this way. Rathe lay flat, pretending to be a log. The Tse'Mara passed high overhead, heading south.

When dawn paled the eastern sky, the throgs stopped and made camp. One stood on watch. The other four were sleeping.

The day was warm but the sky was gray and cloudy. The stalkers moved slowly, carefully. It took them an hour to get into position, crawling on their bellies. Rathe's body was tired, but he felt exhilarated. He glanced at Kel, and saw the same light shining in her eyes. This time they were the hunters. Orvig was grim.

They could see the throg who was standing watch. He had green skin, pointed ears, and no hair. He was about Rathe's height, although he stood slightly bow-legged. He wore crude skins and fur boots, and leaned on a spear. A shortsword was strapped to his side. He was humming quietly to himself.

They struck swiftly. Kel murmured words and threw. Her runespear flew as quickly as any arrow, piercing the sentry's throat. He dropped, gurgling. Rathe and Orvig raced forward. Their swords rose and fell. It was butcher's work. Three throgs died before they woke. The fourth rolled over and drew a long knife, snarling. Orvig dealt him a vicious kick to the head. He collapsed.

Rathe stood panting, covered in gore. Green bodies were scattered about. Orvig looked ill. A weak retching noise came from the throg that Orvig had kicked. Kel smiled, grimly.

Kel searched the corpses, while Orvig and Rathe bound the captive warrior to a tree trunk. Rathe was surprised. The throg was female.

He leaned down, put his sword to her throat. "We want to know a few things," said Rathe slowly. "Do you understand me?"

"Uyasru Makkar ky Rhyanis Une-Makkar." she said. "Wiotha eh

falkarr ni."

Orvig knew a little of the throg tongue — Jhen had practiced on him. He translated: "I be Rhyanis, warrior of the Une-Makkar tribe." He looked at Rathe. "You'll get nothing from me."

"Won't talk?" asked Kel. She stepped out from the shadow of the trees, the soft breeze blowing her black feathered cloak about her. She held her rune spear. The blood still dripped from its tip.

The prisoner craned her head to look, then caught her breath.

"Jedaykeen!" she gasped, voice shaking. "Isas! Keep 'way!"

Kel laughed and stepped forward

"Jedaykeen. What's that mean?" Rathe asked.

"Slithering death that stalks the day," said Orvig. "I think." He looked at Kel. "I don't think she likes you, lass."

"Thank you," said Kel. She rolled it around her tongue, then leaned in close to the throg, and hissed "Jeddaaykeeen."

The hunter turned a pale shade of lime.

Kel grinned, but she let Orvig pull her a step back.

They conferred together a few paces away.

"She's afraid of Kel," Rathe said. "Why?"

"Who knows?" said Kel innocently. "But she does seem fright-ened, doesn't she?"

"Terrified," said Orvig. He looked at Kel. "Was it your head-hunting?"

She shrugged.

"We need to make her talk," Rathe said. "But I won't use tor-ture. We'll try frightening her."

"Huh," said Kel. She nodded at Orvig. "She's your prisoner." She brightened. "We can always kill her if it doesn't work."

Chapter Six

"You'll have to talk to her," Kelandra said to Orvig. "Find out where your Jhen is," she said, "and how we can reach her without getting caught."

Rathe nodded. He was sitting on a tree stump, wiping the blood off his sword with a rag. "And see if you can find out why the throgs started this," added Rathe. He looked at his blade. "If we're killing them, I want to know why."

"I'll do my best, boy," Orvig said. He glanced at Kel. "You stay over there, lass. She's too nervous to talk when you're close."

Orvig approached the captive warrior. His throg-speech was slow and halting. He punctuated his words with gestures, trying to make himself understood. Often he pointed at Kel, and once at Rathe. The throg woman answered in a low voice, almost a whisper, darting furtive glances in Kel's direction.

"Did you find anything on the bodies?" Rathe asked Kelandra.

"Nothing much," Kel replied. She was sorting through a stack of leather helmets, cloaks, coarse tunics and fur breeches they'd stripped from the dead. "Some provisions. I won't touch their meat, but they had some black bread and dried fruit we can use." Kel paused. "And one of the warriors you slew had this." She handed him a shortsword.

Rathe turned it over in his hands, noting the fine workmanship. "This is Dwarven steel," Rathe said. "Not throg-work. It was made in Stonekeep." He studied the inscription on the side. He nodded grimly. "Last year's mark, from the Albenforge clan. It's not some heirloom. They got this off the Seth party."

Orvig came over to them, looking thoughtful.

"Well," he said. "I've found out a fair bit, though I had to promise that Kel here would eat her heart if she didn't tell me."

"Does she speak truth, do you think?" asked Kel.

Orvig nodded. "She's sure we're all magickers — I think she's too scared to lie. She told me her tribe, the Une-Makkar, has a stronghold a half-day's journey from here. They call it Carkulroth — the Sheltering Dark. That's where they took Jhen. By the way, you were right," he said to Kel. "She's being held in a dungeon, in their stronghold. Their Shaman's been questioning her about Stonekeep."

"Why?" said Rathe. "What could he want?"

"Rhyanis doesn't know. She's only an ordinary warrior. But she seems to think," Orvig gave a tight smile, "that we Dwarves control Stonekeep. He wants Jhen to tell him our secrets." Orvig turned somber. "Poor old Hoth was almost right, boy. The throgs *are* preparing for war. Their Shaman has big dreams. And now that they've crushed Kel's folk, he wants to drive out our logging parties, and there's talk of a mass assault on the other forts. From what Rhyanis says, I think this Shaman plans to conquer the entire Vale of Khera. Maybe more."

"The Shaman in his feathered cloak," Rathe said, recalling Kel's words, from just before the magickal attack. "Who is he?"

"Well, the last chief Shaman was an old fellow named Jevaka Raye. He'd been Shaman for years and years. He believed in trade with the human tribes. The occasional skirmish to keep the young bucks happy, but fighting for honor, not territory."

"Yes," said Kel. "Before they tamed the Tse'Mara, throg traders came two or three times a year. I remember the strange smells... foreign spices. They brought thick hides from the mountains, and nuggets of raw gold and copper. But sometimes we'd quarrel over hunting grounds, and our warriors would meet the throgs across a stream. We'd throw spears at each other. When we hit someone, they'd run and give us hunting rights — at least, till next season."

"What if one of your warriors got hurt?"

"Then we'd do the same. Sometimes people got hurt — my uncle Erj was almost killed. Once in a while they'd raid, steal our sheep. And so would we. But it wasn't war. We never even thought of attacking their villages, wiping them out." She glared at the captive throg with hate-filled eyes. "Like they did to us."

"So what happened? Why did Jevaka Raye turn hostile?"

"Gotha Karn happened." Orvig looked grim. "A nasty piece of work, though our friend Rhyanis doesn't want to tell us much. I think she's almost as frightened of him as she is of Kel. Rathe, do you know how throgs choose their chieftains?"

Rathe shook his head.

"Jhen told me once. Through magickal duels. Gotha Karn had magick, but not much. And if you're a throg with any magickal talent at all, it's not safe to hang around a tribe with a real shaman. He might get the idea that you're trying to replace him, and get rid of you first. So you get out of there, if you're smart. Maybe find another tribe that doesn't have a shaman, or maybe just live alone and practice your magick."

"I gather Gotha Karn was smart?"

"He went into exile in the wilds. But then he found something. Our captive's just an ordinary hunter-warrior. She doesn't know the whole tale. But Karn boasted that while he was exiled, he found a ruined temple in the hills. He defeated its guardian, and..." he glanced at Kel.

"And what?" said Kel.

"And took its head."

"The black crystal skull," said Rathe.

"Exactly," said Orvig. "It boosted what powers he already had. It also gave him control over animals — and insects."

"The Tse'Mara," said Rathe.

"The Tse'Mara," echoed Orvig. "They were just wild creatures, before."

"That's right," said Kel. "They lived in the mountains, but they rarely took humans, mostly small game like rabbits or goats. So it was Gotha Karn." She smiled wickedly, and stroked the rune-carved tip of her spear. Now her enemy had a name. "And he used the skull's power to craft runes to control them?"

Orvig nodded. "And now they're his personal pets," he said. "With their help, and whatever other magicks it gave him, he came back and defeated the old Shaman, Jevaka Raye."

"What happened to Jevaka?" Rathe asked.

Orvig shrugged. "Usually the loser is killed in the duel — or right afterward. But Gotha Karn kept the old shaman alive." He glanced back at the captive throg, who was hanging limply in her bonds. "Rhyanis doesn't know why. But they're keeping him in a pit in Carkulroth. Just like Jhen."

They sat down to eat, sharing the throgs' fruit and bread, smearing it with the last of the cheese. Over Kel's objections, Rathe took their captive a drink of water.

"Open up," he told her and tapped his mouth. He mimed drinking. She stared at him for a moment, and Rathe thought he could read in her face a mix of stubborn pride and fear. Then she opened her mouth, and Rathe let her drink from the canteen.

"Trys'neh," she told him, in a flat voice. Was it "thank you?" Or a curse? Rathe shrugged. He went back to join his friends.

They were discussing how to get into Carkulroth. Orvig favored scouting the stronghold — by daylight, when the throgs slept — for hidden entrances. Rhyanis had said she didn't know of any, but Jhen had told him that throg strongholds were riddled with secret passages and hidden portals — bolt holes made by the Shaman and his followers. "Just because Rhyanis doesn't know about them, doesn't mean they're not there," he argued. "If everybody knows about them, they're not secret, now, are they?"

"So, if they're there," said Rathe, "how easy would it be to spot them?"

"That's the hard part," Orvig admitted. "If Carkulroth is as big as Rhyanis says it is, it might cover an acre or more. But I like it better than Kel's plan."

Rathe looked inquiringly at her.

"We become throgs," Kel said.

"That's why you were looking over their clothes?" Rathe asked. She nodded. He frowned, then shook his head. "It might fool them at a distance in bad — I mean good — light. But not up close. And we probably smell different, too."

"She's not talking about an ordinary disguise," Orvig said. "She's talking about using rune magick. I don't like it." He looked unhappy. "Tell Rathe what you'd have to do, Kelandra."

Kelandra explained what the rune-spell involved. It was simple but ruthless; Rathe was appalled. But he could think of nothing else. The throgs they had killed were already dead, he told himself. Jhen wasn't. The rest didn't matter. Over Orvig's objections, he gave Kel his assent.

At Rathe's insistence, they dragged the four throg bodies into the bushes, so they were out of sight of the captive. He could be ruthless, but letting Rhyanis watch what they were about to do, Rathe knew, was beyond cruelty.

Kelandra bent over the first throg corpse. She had spent the last few minutes sharpening her knife.

"It's nothing special," Kel said modestly. "It's one of the first runes I learned. Every shaman knows it. Washoora, the beast-mask. Our hunters used it," Kel said. "To stalk game."

"Aye," said Orvig glumly. "I've heard trader's tales of it. Your hunters dress in a cloak cut from an animal skin. A Shaman draws a rune and an illusion covers the hunter, so he looks like the beast whose skin he wears. But the spell is for animals!"

"Yes," said Kel. "It was, wasn't it?" She smiled, tested the knife's edge on her finger, drew blood. Then she bent to her work.

Orvig looked away. "Jedaykeen," he muttered under his breath.

As afternoon faded into evening, three throg warriors gazed at

the fastness that was Carkulroth. One was a young male, who bore a captured sword of good Dwarven make. The second was a female, carrying a flint-carved spear, its tip wrapped in rags. The third was very short — perhaps he had been stunted at birth, or had some shar-ga blood. Unusual for throgs, the eyes of these three warriors did not blink in the late afternoon sun.

Those eyes looked upon a bleak plateau, broken by jagged out-cropping of yellow and brown stone, bare under a brooding sky. The ground was naked save for scraggly bushes and a few hardy rhododen-drons, cracked in places, strewn with boulders elsewhere. A dirt track wound its way among them.

In its midst squatted a grim fastness... a rude keep built of great blocks of black unmortared stone. The only entrance was a spiked gate of iron-reinforced timber. The walls were topped with rough battlements. No banner fluttered from its towers, nor did they see warriors manning the defenses.

"Most of it's underground," said the small throg, who spoke in the language of Stonekeep, but with a Dwarven accent. "Those works are just to protect the entrance."

"Kyas," agreed the male warrior, whose name was Rathe. It meant "yes," in throg-speech. Orvig had drilled them in a few simple throg phrases, in case they were challenged.

"Ky-AS," the dwarf corrected. "The accent's on the last syllable."

"I'd sooner kill a throg them speak with him," said Kel.

"Try to restrain yourself," Rathe said. "I think we should take cover, rest, and then enter an hour or so before dawn. That way most of the throgs will be tired or getting ready to sleep."

"That sounds good, boy," said Orvig. "Kelandra?"

"Kyas," said Kel, pronouncing it correctly. She stuck her tongue out at Orvig. It was green.

They concealed themselves among boulders and rested, although one of them always kept watch.

Earlier, Kelandra had spent the morning casting the runes that created the shape-masking cloaks. Rathe and Orvig had sealed the captive throg in a makeshift prison, a hillside cave with a heavy boulder pushed over the entrance. Over Kel's protests, the trail rations and spare canteens they'd taken from the dead throgs were left with Rhyanis. They'd last a week, maybe. Rathe hoped he'd be back before then.

Rathe couldn't relax. He tugged at the fastening of the skin cloak he wore. It felt constricting, and the smell was a constant reminder of what it was. Yet he dared not remove it — that would break the rune-spell. It could only be used once. To replace it would take Kel over an hour — not to mention another skin.

To take his mind off it, he watched the throg stronghold. By night, Carkulroth was alive with activity. Soon after dark, several parties had left the stronghold, disappearing into the forest — Rathe guessed most were hunters, for they carried long spears but lacked shields or armor. Twice they heard the beating of wings, and once the moonlight glinted off a half-dozen Tse'Mara. They settled on the battlements like pigeons on a balcony.

Ultimately, gaining entrance proved easier then they thought. Rathe spotted two sizable hunting parties returning at the same time. It was earlier than they'd planned, but he decided to seize the moment. He rousted Orvig and Kelandra, and broke cover. They moved in behind the hunters, mingling with the stragglers as the two parties merged into a single larger group of jostling throgs.

Rathe was tense — he knew he was sweating, and hoped the spell would conceal it. He chanced a glance at Kel: she moved confidently, like a stalking tigress. Being in the stronghold of her enemy didn't discomfit her. She acted like a throg, snarling at one hunter who stepped too close to her, pushing her way through the mass. He tried to imitate her, to move more confidently without drawing attention to himself.

The gate yawned open, and they passed through it. Rathe noted the thickness of the walls: a dozen feet of stone. They entered a timber-roofed corridor that sloped downward. Two guards stood just inside, wearing armor of boiled leather, and bright helmets of beaten copper with their cheeks carved like boar-tusks. They carried wooden shields and steel shortswords, blades Rathe was sure had been taken from dead Stonekeep traders. No password was asked. The guards merely exchanged guttural greetings with the leaders of the hunting party. Rathe nodded at the guards, and was waved through.

The passage ended in a series of deep wells. The hunters ahead of Rathe swarmed into and down them, and Rathe saw that wooden ladders led downward. He hesitated, but Orvig tugged at his arm — deep places held no terror for a dwarf. Kel was already past him. He followed, hand over hand into the dark. Thankfully, it wasn't pitch black. Small lights shone at intervals, tiny sparks that Rathe realized were caged fireflies.

The ladder took Rathe into a wide fire-lit hall. Its walls were of rough-hewn stone, decorated with shields, crossed spears and animal trophies. A half-dozen side passages led from it, and some of the hunters vanished down them. Throgs, bare to the waist, turned haunches of meat over huge fires. Copper cauldrons bubbled over other firepits. The air was filled with the odors of throg cooking: acrid and spicy, but oddly appetizing. A throg in a leather apron shouted instructions to scurrying figures who Rathe first thought were throg children. Then he realized they were shargas, the throg's stunted cousins.

He was blocking traffic. A slim throg, a young female balancing a sloshing urn on her head, jostled into Rathe, and nearly spilled her burden. She stepped back and cringed. He murmured "Skarl" — sorry. She looked startled — maybe proper warriors didn't apologize — then favored him with an appraising glance and a tusky throg smile. He caught Kel looking at him oddly, and with a start, he realized the throg girl had, perhaps, found him attractive.

Most of the hunters had dumped their kills on wood tables or hung them from hooks in the ceiling, then left. Rathe knew he had to keep moving. He looked to Orvig, and the dwarf nodded. They picked a little-trod passage at random and took it. Soon Rathe lost all sense of direction: corridors branched away like fingers from a hand, multiplying into a bewildering labyrinth.

"Rhyanis said this place has at least three levels," said Orvig. "The pits are at the bottom. Look for any ladders or stairs."

The passage they were traveling was narrow, pierced with crude doorways covered with hanging blankets. From behind some came voices, and once what sounded like a blow followed by a yelp. He hesitated beside it — could that be Jhen? — when it flew open and a pair of tiny throg children, naked save for sandals, ran out, holding loaves of bread. They ducked around Rathe, and ran down the corridor. A moment later, an elderly throg stuck his head out the doorway and shook his fist — then noticed Rathe and Kel, paused, muttered "skarl," and backed away.

Rathe grinned sheepishly. They continued on their way.

"Gods, what a maze," Kel said. She shuddered. They'd been walking for some minutes. As they went deeper into Carkulroth, the firefly cages became fewer in number, the dark grew more oppressive. "Are the Dwarves' caverns like this?"

"Somewhat," answered Rathe, "but they are lit by silver lamps, and decorated by hanging tapestries. Not like this gloom."

"Still, this is good stonework," Orvig remarked. He tapped the close-fitting blocks making up the wall. "If they'd..."

He was interrupted by shouts and the sound of many boots, and suddenly the passage was filled with jostling, pushing throgs. The living wave carried Rathe down the corridor, into a side chamber filled with tables and benches, its walls decorated with hunting trophies and crossed spears. The warriors elbowed each other, calling out names and snatches of songs. Most bore drinking horns filled with foaming liquid.

"Une-Makkar-skay!" a throg yelled. There was an answering shout, and a dozen horns were raised in toast.

In the crush, Rathe had lost sight of Orvig. He thought he saw Kel, but it was hard to be sure among so many green, leather-clad bodies. He tried to move in that direction.

A bulky warrior in a copper helmet like those the gate-guards had worn was beside Rathe. He raised his drink and yelled "Ystack! Gotha-skay!"

Several heads turned, but none answered him, and Rathe felt a tension in the room. Had that been a toast to Gotha Karn? The copper-helmed warrior lurched to his feet and glared around him. His eyes came to rest on Rathe beside him. He shoved a drinking horn into Rathe's hand, then splashed liquid into it from a flask. "Ystack yi

Gotha?" he snarled, one fist raised threateningly.

No need for trouble. Rathe lifted the horn and shouted "Gotha-skay!" hoping it made sense. The toast was echoed by the copper-helmed warrior, and by a few others as well — though not by all.

Experimentally, Rathe downed the brew. He nearly choked — it was steaming hot! The copper-helmed warrior laughed and clapped him on the arm, pushing past to sit by him, ignoring what looked like glares from those around him. A second copper-helmeted throg pushed through the crowd and joined him at the table. They conversed in low tones. Rathe tried to listen, but he could understand little throg-speech. He caught one or two words — *Tse'Mara* was one, *Gotha* another — but no meaning.

Rathe pretended to sip his drink, and looked about, seeking his companions in the press of bodies. There was still no sign of Orvig — but from somewhere behind him he heard what sounded like Kelandra's voice, raised in urgent tones.

He whirled about, spotted her. "Ay, Ay!" she was saying — throg-speech for "No!" A tall throg had grabbed hold of her, was trying to plant wet kisses on her face. Kel was struggling, breathing hard. The throg reached for Kel's cloak, to tear it away.

That would break the rune spell! Without thinking, Rathe stepped forward, grabbed the over-amorous throg by the collar and yanked him back. The warrior fell heavily against the floor with a crash, his drinking-horn splashing Rathe with hot brew. The throg shook his head, stunned, and stared up dumbly.

A dozen heads turned. Trouble!

"M'tar!" shouted Rathe, exhausting his store of throg speech. *Mine!* He drew Kel roughly into his arms and kissed her full on the mouth, then took a swig of his drink. "M'tar!" he repeated. He hoped he looked and sounded like a drunken, jealous lover. Kel helped, wrapping her arms tightly about him. She snarled down at the throg on the floor, then grinned up at Rathe.

It worked — there was laughter, not threats, and the heads turned away. The copper-helmed throg who'd given Rathe the drink slapped him on the back. Two others helped the downed throg to his feet, then passed him a fresh drink. Holding Kel tightly — it was strange to feel her lithe shape under the throg disguise — Rathe shouldered his way to the edge of the crowd.

They found Orvig waiting just outside the chamber, tapping his foot. He looked none the worse for wear. He noticed Rathe's drink-splashed tunic, Kelandra's disarrayed clothes, and raised an eyebrow.

"Didn't stay for the party?" said Rathe lightly. He was still breathing hard. It had been close. Kel pressed his hand and smiled at him, then stepped back and smoothed her clothes back into shape. Rathe looked right, then left. They were in a narrow hallway lined with doorways. "Come on, let's go," Rathe said.

They came to a bend, heard more shouts and noise coming along one passage, took the other. It seemed to slant downwards. They followed it for several minutes. Twice they saw single throgs run by, stripped to loincloths and wearing coarse yellow scarves about their necks. "Are they messengers?" he asked Orvig. The dwarf shrugged — he didn't know.

The trio took a side passage. Ahead, they heard the hiss of fabric on stone, grunting voices cursing. It was a trio of skinny throgs in ragged clothes, dragging heavy sacks. Before Rathe could pull him back, Orvig stepped in front of them. The throg workers stopped, looking nervously at each other.

"Hroi, makkar-brotah," Orvig hailed them. *Good night, kinsman,* Rathe knew that was. Orvig slurred his words as if drunk to cover any deficiencies in his accent. "Yi te'sriech po — ah, podor?" Rathe wasn't sure what the rest meant, only that it was a question.

One of them scratched his head. "Skarl," he said. "Yi podor mistrach." He waved down a side passage. "Yi podor rukos nu."

"Kyas," said Orvig. He gestured at Rathe to follow, and he and Kel did so. The throgs stepped aside to let them pass.

They turned right, and Rathe could feel a faint draft. They found themselves in a small chamber with a stairway leading down.

"You asked directions?" Kel asked the dwarf.

"Aye," Orvig said. He gestured. "The pits are down this way, past a storeroom." He frowned. "They seemed edgy."

"Maybe they thought you were drunk and mean," Kel said. She

looked down on him, patted his head. "A pint-sized warrior like you's got to be twice as nasty, right?"

Orvig gave her an irritated glare. "It was more than that," he told her. "Perhaps no one likes to talk about the dungeons."

They followed the stairwell down. It led down a long way, past a landing, and then into a small chamber with three passages branching out of it. A well stood in the middle, a bucket beside it. Orvig sniffed the water. "It should be safe," he said, and took a short drink. The others followed suit.

"Which way?" asked Rathe.

"He said the left passage," Orvig answered. He led them down it. The stonework here seemed rougher, more natural. The passage was dark and poorly lit, and they were taken by surprise when it suddenly widened into a cavernous chamber filled with wooden barrels, Rathe banging into one of them. It sloshed slightly.

They looked about, found a wooden doorway. A faint light showed under it.

"The dungeons?" said Kel.

"It's in the right place," Orvig answered.

"Careful," warned Rathe. "There may be guards we can't talk our way past."

Orvig put his ear to the door, listened, then motioned Rathe over and unfastened his pack. As Rathe and Kel watched, the dwarf carefully looked through the many bottles and implements there. After what seemed like hours, his stubby fingers seized a small vial. He uncorked it, and dripped a thick liquid over the door's hinges.

"Oil," Orvig said. "So it won't squeak. Open it just a crack."

Rathe did, slowly and carefully, a hairline crack. The door opened noiselessly. He peered through.

The chamber was squarish, about ten paces on a side, lit by the glow of a shielded brazier filled with hot coals. There was a closed wooden door at the far end. Beside it stood a slim, youthful throg dressed in close-fitting brown leather. He wore a dark cowl over his head, his ears protruding from it. He was speaking with one of the copper-helmeted warriors that Rathe was beginning to think of as Gotha's Guards. The warrior was gesturing at the floor, pointing at a trap-door, one of five evenly spaced about the room. Rathe couldn't make out his words, though.

He moved his head slightly, trying to take in the entire room through the narrow crack. Two other copper-helmed guards were seated around a low table, ignoring the conversation. They were scratching designs into it the tabletop with knives, concentrating on them. A pitcher of water and a half-eaten loaf of bread sat on the table beside them, and after a moment, Rathe guessed they were playing some kind of game.

Behind the guards' table was a cross-shaped wooden frame, its sides pitted and stained. Beside it Rathe saw a long coil of coarse rope, a bucket, and a many-thonged whip. He shuddered, guessing at their purpose.

He felt a tap on his shoulder. It was Kelandra. He pulled back, letting Kel and Orvig take their own turns. Orvig stayed for a long while. After a moment, Rathe saw his friend's shoulders were shaking.

They moved back from the door, and took cover behind a barrel. "What is it?" Rathe asked. "Did you hear what they were saying?"

"Curse them," said Orvig. He turned to Rathe, eyes burning. "The cowled throg came from Gotha Karn. The Shaman is impatient. The prisoners' rations are halved. Again." Orvig stressed the last word. "The guard told him they'd already halved them once. If they fed them any less, they'll eat each other." Orvig slammed his fist into his palm. "Then they both laughed."

"We'll get her out," Rathe said. "Don't worry."

Rathe and Orvig conferred in low voices. In the end, they could come up with nothing more clever than a frontal attack. They would try to freeze the guards with a shout, kill them all, and take their clothing. With luck, the copper helms would be symbols of authority that would let them get outside. As they spoke, Kel remained silent, simply nodding in agreement. Rathe wondered what she was thinking. He remembered the feel of her against him, when they'd kissed.

He took Kel's hand. She looked up. "Be careful," he told her.

Kel smiled, nodded. "You too." She grinned. "Don't worry. I'm the Jedaykeen."

Orvig and Rathe drew their blades, and Kel unwrapped the rags that covered the runes on her spear's tip.

"Ready?" said Orvig.

Rathe nodded.

"Now!"

Orvig kicked the door open and charged, shouting "Jhen!" The other two followed on his heels, yelling wordlessly, maniacally.

The companions were across the room before the throgs could draw their weapons. But though the guards were surprised, they were good. One of them shouted, and kicked the table over at Kelandra. It overturned, sending the pitcher of water shattering on the stone floor. Kel jumped back, and then the throg had his own sword out.

Orvig and the other guard were locked in a duel of flashing blades. The throg had the edge on reach, but Orvig seemed filled with a demonic energy. The throg shouted loudly and attacked. Orvig parried the stroke, feinted at the throg's head, then slashed at his wrist. He cut too low, and the blade sliced away two fingers instead. Dark blood spurted.

Kel thrust with her spear, holding it two-handed. Her foe parried and fell back. Kel stepped over the fallen table, advancing cautiously. She knew she had the reach on him.

Rathe faced two throgs, but the cowled youth seemed armed only with a knife. The guard with him had been looking the other way when they burst in. He whirled, eyes widening at the sight of Rathe's charge. Perhaps he would have drawn his sword in time, but then the cowled throg yelled... and shoved his companion, impaling him on Rathe's sword! They went down in a tumble of limbs. The cowled throg turned and ran for the door.

The warrior facing Orvig dropped his sword, clutching his ruined hand. Orvig followed through with a hard upthrust into the stomach. The throg went down, clutching at his belly.

Rathe gasped for breath. The warrior atop him was a dead weight, unmoving. He looked up, and saw the other door squeak closed. The cowled throg was getting away! He cursed feelingly, shoved the body away, and struggled to his feet, trying to tug his blade free of his foe's ribs.

Kel's foe looked wildly about, and saw both his friends were down. His ears flattened and he charged with a berserk yell. Kel braced herself and spitted him neatly through the breast, her rune-tipped spear piercing the boiled leather armor with ease.

Orvig stood panting, holding his bloody sword. Jhen! He grabbed the coil of rope, then examined the trap doors in the floor. Four were unbolted. The fifth was locked shut. He slid the bolt open and looked down. The pit was seven feet deep, and stank. A small niche halfway up held an oil lamp. Its pitiless light illuminated two faces staring hopelessly upwards. The only furnishing was a reeking slop-bucket.

Rathe ran to the door and opened it. It led into a long corridor. Twenty paces down its length he saw the black-cowled throg — and he wasn't alone; a half-dozen warriors surrounded him. He pointed at Rathe and shouted something. Rathe could guess what it was.

Orvig looked down into the pit. One prisoner was a throg, his green face pale and wrinkled with great age, his body thin and frail. Had he been a human, he might have been seventy or eighty. As it was, Orvig could not guess his age. His eyes were — with a start, Orvig realized he was blind. His eyes were empty sockets, surrounded by charred flesh.

The second — Orvig's heart leaped. It was Jhen. Her youthful face was dirty and tear-streaked, eyes red with lack of sleep. Her clothes were rags. But it was his sister. It was Jhen.

She looked up, squinting, then shrank back, as if afraid.

"Jhen!" Orvig shouted.

The girl paused, startled to hear her name. *What have they done to her?* Orvig thought. *She doesn't know me!* He slapped his forehead, then tore off the rune-cloak. "Jhen, it's me," he called.

The dwarf-girl put her hand to her mouth. "Orvig?" she said wonderingly. She rubbed her eyes. "It *is* you!"

"Jhen!" he called. "I've come to get you." He lowered down the rope. "Catch."

"Orvig!" she shouted. Then she turned to her cellmate, who had watched Orvig with his sightless eyes. "Please, you have to help him, too." She tied the rope around the throg's waist.

Rathe ducked back into the room. "You've found her?"

Orvig only grunted. He and Kel had tied the rope about the table, and Orvig was straining against the rope, pulling.

A head popped into view. It wasn't Jhen — it was an old throg. Rathe stared. Was this Jevaka Raye, the ancient shaman?

There was no time to waste.

"Kel, help me! Bring the table to brace the door. We can build a barricade and — " He heard running footsteps, stuck his head out the door. A half-dozen warriors were charging up the corridor. "Gods! There's no time!" He glanced back at Orvig. He was straining at the rope again, the old throg helping him. At least he was good for something, Rathe thought. "Hurry!"

Rathe drew his sword, prepared to meet them just inside the doorway. Kel moved to stand by his side.

Eight throgs charged. They had shields and light armor. Rathe could see the cowled youth behind them, urging them on.

Suddenly, Kel cast off her cloak. Rathe did the same. The onrushing throgs halted in disarray, suddenly faced by the apparition of two human warriors. Rathe shouted and charged, Kel right behind him. Caught by surprise, two throgs fell in as many seconds. Rathe grabbed a fallen shield.

Rathe shouted. "Orvig" he shouted. "Take Jhen and run!" He parried a blow, ducked and thrust. "Hurry! If you get out, meet at the cave!"

Orvig gave a final heave. His sister popped out of the well and into his arms. She stood beside him, hugging him.

He heard Rathe's shout over the clash of blades.

"No time for that," he said. He paused, his hand on his sword. Rathe needed him...

He felt a hand on his arm. It was the old shaman.

"Your friends are warriors," he said, voice a harsh whisper, words strangely accented but understandable. "You cannot help them now. Your sister needs you. She will not escape without you. You came down the stairway?"

"Yes," said Orvig. "We'll try to reach it."

"We must make for it. The landing there..."

"I know, damn you!" Orvig shouted. He hesitated briefly, then looked at the door. Cursing, weeping, he led Jhen and ran from the room, into the warehouse. The shaman stumbled behind.

Rathe fought on, though the corridor ahead was alive with throgs. He thrust and parried, his sword-arm leaden, his shield-arm numb. The buckler he had grabbed was hacked nearly to bits, but it had done its work well — he had yet to take a wound. Kel had been less lucky — blood dripped from a long, shallow cut along her thigh, and Rathe could tell she was slowing.

He glanced sideways at her. Her spear darted like a snake's tongue, stabbing in and out. Though she had no shield, she turned blows deftly, using her spear as though it were a quarterstaff to block sword and axe blows. Together, they gave ground slowly, making the throgs pay for every foot. But even so, they had been forced back into the doorway of the dungeon chamber.

At least Orvig got away, Rathe told himself. *And Jhen. They still have a chance.*

Orvig kept urging Jhen to move faster. His sister was falling behind, slowing herself to help the blind old throg. Every so often he stopped, listening. He still thought he could hear shouts, the clash of arms. Against hope, he prayed Rathe and Kel would make it, that something — Rathe's skill, Kel's magick — would be enough to make a difference. That they would get away.

There was no rest for Rathe. Reinforcements had come, but for the wrong side. The first throg warriors had fled or fallen, replaced by copper-helmeted elite guards, armed with shields and steel swords. The last minute of fighting had claimed few casualties — they had wounded some more throgs, but had been unable to press their own attacks. The warriors they faced were more skilled, and injured guards had simply fallen back, allowing fresh warriors to take their places. He and Kel had no such respite. They had been forced back into the chamber, and now stood back to back, surrounded. There was no place to retreat, no place to run.

Through the circle of warriors, Rathe glimpsed the visage of the cowled, youthful throg, the one who had killed one of his own warriors to escape Rathe. Now his pale green face was smiling, his cold eyes gazing at Rathe and Kel as if he already possessed them. Then he turned away, shouting orders in a calm voice, calling more soldiers into the fray.

Kel saw him, too. Hate boiled within her, mingling with the pain of her wound. She wished she dared to cast her spear — he was obviously a leader of some sort. But then she would fall, and there would be no one to guard Rathe's back.

They had reached the stairs, pounding upwards. The old throg had his hand pressed to his side, and seemed to be in pain.

"Brother," Jhen panted, "Are there many more stairs?"

Orvig nodded. "But there's a landing coming up," he added. "We'll rest there a moment."

He could hear no sounds of pursuit — not yet, anyway. He pushed that thought away. Pursuit would mean that Rathe...

Now Rathe stood alone. Kel lay on the ground, a broken spear protruding from her shoulder. Blood pooled beneath her. Unconscious or dead, Rathe couldn't tell.

"Alive," hissed their cowled leader. "Take him alive." Rathe could not understand the words, but he guessed their meaning.

A wave of new throgs came, armed with shields and clubs. Rathe raised his sword. The foe broke over him like a green tide.

Jhen's own breath came in great gasps. Confined for nearly a week, she was in poor shape to run. But they dared not stop.

They reached the landing. Jhen collapsed on the floor. The old throg dropped to his knees, hugging himself, then dragged himself to his feet. Orvig leaned against the wall.

But they couldn't rest. They could hear the pursuit now —

shouts coming from below. He turned to Jhen, shook her shoulder. *No more lying to myself,* he thought. *We won't make it.*

He drew his sword.

A withered pale-green hand fell on his shoulder. Blind eyes turned to meet his own.

"Wait, Jhen's brother," said the old voice. "I have a better way."

Chapter Seven

Rathe awoke in darkness, his wounds afire, to the feel of cold, wet stone against his body. He was curled into a fetal position, and he ached everywhere, a mass of cuts and bruises. The worst was his shield-arm — he winced when he touched it. It wasn't broken, but it felt like a bone bruise.

He remembered the fight, the sight of Kelandra going down, her high scream as a spear pierced her shoulder. What happened next had been almost welcome, after that scream.

But now he lived. And he did not know if Kel did. Or Orvig.

Wincing, he staggered to his feet. The ceiling was too high to touch, the walls close. He was in a small cell only an arm-span across... perhaps the very one they had rescued Jhen from.

He was alone. He had never been alone before, not like this. The stone walls muffled every sound. The only thing in the cell was a wooden bucket of tepid water. There was no room to stretch out.

He thought of ways to escape, made ingenious plans, but in the end, they all depended on him leaving the cell. He could feel no doorway, and any roof hatch was too high for him to reach.

He tried yelling. He called for Kelandra, and Orvig, and even

Jhen. He shouted insults at his captors, cursed his jailers and Gotha Karn. He got no answer. He expected none. He stopped when his throat became too hoarse to speak.

Hours passed.

He played the battle out in his mind, move by move, thought of different things he might have done, tactics that did not end with Kelandra of Adra lying bleeding at his feet.

He beat the stone walls until his right hand was bloody.

More time passed. Eventually he sat, wrapping his arms about his knees, and tried to sleep. *Sleep was like death,* he thought. Eventually, it came.

Rathe woke. In the blackness of the cell, he had no idea how much time had passed. His wounds still ached, but not as badly. His knuckles hurt — he remembered what he had done. He no longer felt tired, although his stomach rumbled and his throat was parched. He drank the remaining water in the bucket, then used it to relieve himself.

He thought of Kelandra. Orvig might have survived. Orvig was a survivor. But Kelandra — he had seen her fall. And the throgs — they hated her. If she had lived, what would they do to her? There had to be a way to help her. If she was alive, was in a cell like this, what would she be doing? Something magickal, he guessed...

He curled up on the cold floor. What could *he* do? They had taken his sword and dagger, his helmet, even his boots. All he had left was the coarse throg tunic and breeches. He looked at his finger. Even his mother's ring was gone. Did it now adorn some throg's finger? It had been the focus of what little magick power he might have inherited. Without it, without weapons, he was helpless.

He closed his eyes, thought of his mother. She had vanished on a nameless quest — had she too perished in some bleak pit on the edge of the world? Would he ever know? The ring was the only thing left of her. He imagined the rune, Thera's rune. Where was it now, he thought? He could see it in his mind, unflawed, bright, intricate, the temple in his dream, the ring, black obsidian and gold, a heavy weight curled about his finger.

Rathe opened his eyes. Unbelieving, he stared at his right hand. The ring. It was back on his finger. He had called it back!

He had little time to think about it — suddenly there was a loud crash above him. The ceiling opened, and a faint radiance spilled down. Light! Rathe looked up. And was met with a wash of ice-cold water that almost knocked him to his knees.

Shivering with cold, Rathe cursed and was rewarded with throg laughter. But instead of slamming the trapdoor shut, they threw down a rope. "Char!" a voice commanded. Rathe didn't know the word, but the meaning was crystal clear. Ignoring the pain in his limbs, he climbed. As he neared the top, rough hands reached for him, and he yelped as they touched his bruises.

He stood in a chamber, surrounded by a dozen copper-helmed bullies. They twisted his arms behind his back, tying them with a coarse length of rope. "Az nab!" one of them ordered, shoving him. He nearly fell, but regained his balance.

The throgs guarding him spoke little, though he recognized a few words. "Jevaka Raye" was repeated several times, in nervous tones, and once he heard "Warrow," which he thought Orvig had said meant "dwarf." They didn't seem to be talking about him. He tried to say something in his halting throg-speech, but was rewarded by a sharp blow across the mouth.

Then he was force-marched through winding corridors and up two flights of stairs. Down a wide corridor, where curious faces peeped from curtained doorways, but drew back when the guards glared at them. Finally, he stood in front of an open archway, flanked by two hulking warriors. They bore long spears and shields, and wore leather armor sewn with iron scales. Full helms covered their faces, shaped to resemble the heads of Tse'Mara. As the party approached, they crossed their spears to bar the entrance.

"Sul ab Gotha Karn," came the challenge, slightly muffled by the guard's mask.

"Skas yi az Gotha Karn!" answered the warrior holding Rathe's arm.

The spears lifted. Rathe was marched through.

Rathe was dragged into a wide hall, its walls covered with shields, weapons and the skulls of great animals — bears and wolves, stags and great cats, mutant forest creatures that had no names. Tables were shoved against either wall, and seated on benches were a score of copper-helmed warriors. Their heads swivelled to stare at Rathe as he entered. At the far end of the room a third table stood facing the door, on a raised platform. At it sat two warriors, both wearing the full-helmed insect masks, though these were pushed back so Rathe could see the throg faces under them. Between them sat the hooded youthful throg who had directed the battle. He gazed down at Rathe, face twisted into a mocking smile. But he seemed nothing more than a cruel child, overshadowed by the figure seated next to him.

Rathe stared, knowing he saw his enemy face to face.

"I am Gotha Karn, Shaman and war-chief of the Une-Makkar, master of the Whispering Death." The speaker was a throg of middle years, tall but very thin, his skin stretched like parchment over his skull. The throg's eyes were oval, almost too large for his narrow face. He wore a white cloak of eagle feathers, spotted with red stains, and around his neck was a sun-shaped amulet of beaten gold. In one hand he held a staff — and Rathe stared, for atop the staff was mounted a life-sized skull, a head carved from black glass. Its forehead was carved with the same rune that marked the Tse'Mara.

Gotha Karn tilted his head sideways, exchanged a whisper with the coiled youth beside him. Then he leaned forward.

"My son Parlock tells me you led the warriors who attacked Carkulroth." With a gesture, he waved back the men holding Rathe. "Approach me, outlander. Give me your name."

"I am Rathe of Stonekeep, acting Watchmaster of Fort Thunder," Rathe replied. "Where are my comrades?"

"The female?" Gotha Karn said. There was a whisper, a susurrus of voices. Rathe thought he heard the word "Jedaykeen" whispered back and forth. But Gotha Karn raised his hand, and there was silence.

"Is she your mate, then?" When Rathe gave no answer, he

paused, and studied Rathe's face. "I thought so. Well, Rathe of Stonekeep, she still lives," Karn said. "Whether she continues to do so, depends on you. Do you understand?"

"I hear you," said Rathe.

"When my Tse'Mara first spotted your spies trespassing in my lands, I was filled with wrath."

"Spies?" said Rathe, outraged. "You mean our traders?"

"Spies," repeated Gotha Karn. "Though some of my counselors were cowardly, urging me not to strike — they remembered battles in years gone by, when your dwarf-armed warriors bested ours. But those fools were living in the past, a time before Gotha Karn."

"Ah, yes, the Tse'Mara," said Rathe casually. The speech had given him time to regain his composure. "I suppose your creatures were good enough against unsuspecting traders. But our soldiers dealt with them easily enough."

Gotha Karn started to snarl, but then he laughed. "Rathe of Stonekeep, I recognize you, you know! It was you who rallied your warriors, and drove off my Whispering Death, was it not?" He paused, and stroked the crystal skull. "Yes, I watched you. I was looking through my creatures' eyes as they died. I thought I'd killed you then, but it seems you lived. Well. But there are few left of your war-band now, are there? Where are the others? Dead, perhaps? You and that foolish dwarf are the only ones left."

Rathe hung his head, but inside he felt grim satisfaction. He'd learned what he wanted to know. The Shaman didn't know that Tam, Quin and Loric had survived! Whatever happened, Stonekeep would be warned against the Whispering Death. And Orvig — it sounded like he was still free...

"He still eludes you, then?" Rathe hazarded.

"The Dwarves? They won't get far. Dwarves are like rats — hiding in dark places comes naturally to them. But they are little danger." He stared at Rathe. "At first I thought to feed you to the Tse'Mara, you know," the Shaman said conversationally, "but I was impressed by your bravery as a warrior, ineffectual as it was. You sent three of my guards to throgi's halls, and four others will never fight again."

"A shame," said Rathe.

Karn made a dismissive gesture. "If they lost to a pair of humans, I do not need them. But in defeating them, you showed yourself a worthy adversary, Rathe of Stonekeep." He laughed, high and mocking. "Maybe your people are worthy of honor." He eyed Rathe. "What do you say to that, Rathe of Stonekeep?"

"You are right in that," said Rathe. He turned Gotha's words over in his mind, unsure what game the Shaman was playing. "My people have honor."

"Good, good," said Gotha. "It is well to have agreement. But I must be sure. And my people must have proof."

"What kind of proof?" asked Rathe warily, sensing a trap.

Gotha turned to his warriors.

"This is Rathe of Stonekeep," he told them, speaking first in his own language, then repeating his words so that Rathe could understand them. "One of their war-chieftains. Are the people of Stonekeep worthy to be our allies? Or crawling worms, to be crushed? What shall we do?"

"Te il atua j'Isroth!" one of the copper-helmed guards shouted. The cry was taken up by the others.

"Aye, the Trial of throgi," said Gotha. "If the outlander proves himself worthy, I shall send him forth as an emissary, to deliver our words to the stone-dwellers! If they wish our friendship, they must acknowledge our dominion over the Vale of Khera, and pay us tribute to cut our trees! But if he dies, we will know the folk of the Keep are as weak as the villagers, fit only to be slaves, or fodder for the Tse'Mara. What say you, my warriors?"

"Gotha," they chanted. "Kyas j'Isroth!" *Yes, the trial!*

"What is this Trial of throgi?" said Rathe suspiciously.

"A simple one of skill and bravery, I think," said Gotha in a soothing voice. "You must face a beast of the forest, armed only with a short blade." He turned to his son, whispered something. The coiled youth grinned, and scurried away.

"What beast?" said Rathe. His stomach sank. "One of your Tse'Mara?"

"Do you think I am unfair, Rathe of Stonekeep?" He laughed, knowing Rathe's answer. "No, you face a lesser beast. Take him to the circle."

Two warriors grabbed his arms. "Wait, O Karn!" Rathe shouted. "What of the Dwarves and Kelandra? If I pass this test, they must go free too!"

There was sudden silence.

Gotha stroked the black skull and pursed his lips. "Very well," he said at length. "The two Dwarves are spies, but harmless. As for that girl — if you slay the beast, you may take her back with you. We shall not harm her. You have my oath-word."

"Thank you, great Karn," said Rathe. He let out a deep breath. Would Gotha break a promise made in front of his men? He hoped not. He would try his best to win. But what was this beast?

To Rathe's surprise, his guards didn't take him to the Circle immediately. Rather, he was led to a small room, and there given a sip of water and a few scraps of dry bread. He was kept there for a long time, then led away and manhandled up a ladder. He felt a breeze blowing through his hair. With a start, Rathe realized he was outside, in Carkulroth's courtyard.

Overhead, the waning moon stood three-quarters full, enthroned by stars. Its light glinted on the blades of the warriors surrounding him — and on the wings of a dozen Tse'Mara, who watched from their perches atop the battlements.

But there was more than moonlight in the courtyard; a strange pale glow was visible somewhere up ahead. The Shaman sat on a short tripod. In his left hand he held the crystal skull. The glow radiated from the skull's eyes: a silver light, bright as a full moon.

As they dragged him forward, Rathe concentrated on the crystal skull, bringing his mage-sight to bear on it — and staggered.

He shrieked, and dropped to his knees. Sharp pain in his neck. A sense of dislocation. A soul-felt agony of loss, of separation, of humiliation. "Stop!" Rathe shouted. Thinking he had been screaming in terror, the throgs laughed and dragged him on. Rathe tore his gaze away. It ended. He gasped for breath and opened his eyes.

He found himself standing on the lip of a pit, lit by the skull's silver glow. It was about a half-dozen paces across and ten feet deep, its floor covered with packed earth. And within it — Rathe caught his breath. He was looking at a wedge-shaped head nearly as big as his own. Its mottled scales glistened coldly. The green slit-pupiled eyes met his gaze, and held it, unblinking. The head sat atop a coiled body, as thick as his leg, and nearly twenty feet long.

It was a giant serpent.

Rathe thought back to the snakeskin he and Orvig had found outside Alda. The pattern was similar — it could easily have been shed by this monster.

Across the circle, the wind carried Gotha Karn's laughter. Beside him, Rathe could see Parlock grinning, as if at some private joke. Then the Shaman raised his hand, and Rathe felt his bonds being severed. A spear jabbed his back, and he was shoved forward. Rather than topple, he jumped, landing bent-kneed on the packed earth.

"What about the sword?" he shouted.

Gotha nodded. A warrior leaned forward, tossed a blade to him hilt-first. Rathe caught it. He nodded approvingly. It was a deadly tool: a bone-handled iron sword with a heavy stabbing blade. Not steel, but still sharp. But against that snake?

He would do it. For Kelandra. And maybe even for Stonekeep, if pandering to Gotha Karn's ego could help stop a war.

Rathe edged around slowly. Above him, the wind groaned. No, not the wind: the throgs had begun a low, sing-song chant, a deep moaning sound. The snake heard it too. It hissed, and swayed slightly, forked tongue flickering in and out, as if reluctant to attack. Perhaps the sound disoriented it, Rathe thought.

How should he fight a giant snake? Was it poisonous? If it was, a single scratch could mean the end. If not — if it was just a constrictor — it would seek to bite anyway, to hold him while the coils crushed his life out. Either way, then, it would try to bite. He would have to stab at the head while it struck at him.

Rathe decided he would aim for the eye, or failing that, for the tongue. The scales might be tough to penetrate. He rocked forward on the balls of his feet. The packed earth was slightly slippery, but with bare feet, not dangerously so.

The snake seemed reluctant to attack. Rathe stepped in and lunged for the eyes, hoping to find a weak point. The snake dodged, but only just, his blade passing inches from the arching neck. It coiled above him, hissing like one of Orvig's steam kettles. Rathe leapt back, guessing it would strike. But instead it circled, weaving to the left.

Again, Rathe attacked, feinting for its head, then spinning sideways to slash at its neck. But once more it outguessed him, sliding out of range, weaving about him, elegant as a dancer.

There was something almost hypnotic about its movements, and with a start, Rathe realized it was playing with him, not attacking, trying to tire him out. He looked into its unblinking emerald eyes, and nodded. *Creature of the forests,* he asked it silently, *have you hunted men or throgs before, ere the throgs took you for their sport? We are alike in this. But one of us must die!*

Rathe circled it, slowly, the point of his blade extended, making cautious, probing attacks. It dodged them easily, but now Rathe was learning its pattern, the steps of the sinuous dance it wove about him. He almost had it, and he raised his blade *knowing* that it would move just so, and he would strike *then*, and it would die.

And suddenly the pattern was clear.

A dance. Rathe's mind floated back, to the hut in the village, to Kel, interweaving her dance with the serpent Akeshi. And Rathe knew. He stepped forward, but instead of using his sword, he struck with the finger of his right hand, his ring finger. He held a vision of Thera's rune burning in his mind, and he willed, not to see, but to restore!

The body of the snake flowed like water, and became Kel.

She stood in front of him, her dark hair flowing about her like a cloak, emerald eyes sparkling.

Rathe dropped his sword and took her into his arms. Then, together they turned to face the Shaman, Gotha Karn.

"It didn't work, Karn," Rathe shouted. "Your illusion failed. You wanted me to kill her! What of your oath?"

"I promised I would not harm her if you won," the Shaman said. He forced a laugh. "If *you* killed her, what is that to me? But you have failed the test. The snake, the Jedaykeen still lives. Unless you'd like to kill her now."

"The snake is gone, O Karn!" cried Rathe angrily. "I saw your trick and I dispelled it with one blow! Where is *your* honor, O Karn?

The throg warriors murmured. Did Rathe hear agreement in their voices?

"Kill her now, and go free!" cried Karn angrily. "Or die!"

"I'd rather die," said Rathe. He felt Kel's arms tighten around him.

"Very well," said Gotha Karn. He turned to his son. "Parlock, take them back to the pits. I want a suitable demise planned for them, for tomorrow's feast." He grinned. "Be imaginative, or you'll be joining them." The Shaman stood.

"Kyas," said Parlock. He gestured. The warriors closed in.

The cell, barely big enough for one, was cramped with both of them in it. Rathe didn't mind. Gently, he touched Kel's shoulder. There was no sign of a wound.

"Don't worry," said Kelandra. "I won't break."

"You're all right," Rathe said wonderingly. "But the spear wound!"

"Haven't you guessed?" Kel said bitterly. "My secret."

"The snake," Rathe said slowly. "It wasn't an illusion after all, was it?"

"No," Kel answered. She turned her face away. "I'm accursed. A shapeshifter. A weresnake." She grimaced. "Jedaykeen," she said. "Slithering Terror. We heal fast, when we change shape."

"It doesn't matter," Rathe said. Gently, he took her face in his hands, turned her to face him. He kissed her. She responded.

They didn't speak for a long time after that. Then they slept.

"I was the Shaman's daughter, you see," Kel told him. She had begun talking soon after they awakened. She was nestled in his arms, and he stroked her hair as she spoke. "I had the power, and had been trained from childhood. But I made a mistake. I got arrogant. There was a youth from Gothmeg, older than me, I liked him, but he had his own lover. I used my magick to change his feelings about her. But my spell was too strong. His love twisted to hate. He — hurt her."

"Oh, Kel," said Rathe. He hugged her. "You were how old then?"

"Fifteen," Kel said. "It's easy to be jealous when you're young."

"The Shaman found out. I was brought before the village elders. They said I'd acted like a serpent. Some wanted to kill me. Stone me to death. But a wandering priestess was visiting. A priestess of Thera, strong in rune magick. You can guess the rest."

"Kel — this Theran priestess?" Rathe asked. He stopped, not daring to hope. "Was it...?"

"Yes. Her name was Rhea. She must have been your mother. I only met her for a few hours. I never saw her again. But I guess I owe her my life."

"After that, I was an exile. I lived outside the village. Then the Tse'Mara came. You know the rest."

"How often do you change?" Rathe asked.

"For years and years, I was a snake all the time. Rathe, I was fifteen when you were a baby! The snake body... it doesn't anger, and it doesn't age. Rhea put me there to learn patience. Oh, love, I needed that lesson. As I mastered myself, I learned to master my shape as well. Now it's only during a full moon that I have trouble holding human form. That's why I ran away, that first time we met. It was my skin you found." She frowned. "Gotha Karn used his rune-skull to force me to change. And you broke it with Thera's rune."

"Yes," said Rathe. "That skull — it's connected with Thera somehow." Rathe hesitated, then went on. "Your curse was crafted by a Theran priestess. My mother! And the ring, the skull, the image of the Tse'Mara — all versions of the rune on the floor of the great temple, the temple in my dream."

"It could be," said Kel. "But that temple — you saw it ruined, the rune breaking, shattering?"

"Yes," said Rathe. "But listen: the throg girl said Gotha Karn took the skull from an ancient temple. I think it's the same one. A temple of Thera. And because Thera's rune is broken, it can be defiled. And its powers twisted and stolen by Gotha Karn."

Kelandra frowned.

"What?" said Rathe.

"I just realized something," Kel said. "It's been quite a while. Aren't we late for our execution?"

As if to punctuate her words, the walls shook slightly, and they heard a muffled crash.

"Earthquake!" Rathe shouted. Raised in Stonekeep, he knew no greater terror.

"Wait," said Kel. "That didn't feel like a quake." She sniffed. "I smell smoke."

The trapdoor creaked open. Smoke was everywhere. Through the fumes, they saw a green face — a throg wearing a leather helmet and a yellow neck scarf. He peered down. "Li-uasru ki Rathe?" he shouted. He swiped at the vapor, coughing.

Rathe tried to reply, but choked in the smoke. He settled for a vigorous nod.

The throg coughed again, grinned, and lowered down a rope.

By the time they had climbed out, the smoke was slowly clearing. The door to the prison chamber seemed to have been blown off its hinges, as if by a mighty wind. Splinters of charred wood mingled with bodies and parts of bodies. Rathe saw dented copper helmets, and guessed the dead were Gotha Karn's guards. But there were half a dozen live throgs in the room, males and females, of all ages. Some of their rescuers wore armor, others had none. They had one thing in common: they wore yellow scarves and carried swords, spears and axes, and all had a grim light in their eyes. A red-stained bandage was wrapped about the leader's shoulder. It didn't seem to bother him. Rathe recognized him as one of the partying throgs — one of those who had refused to toast Gotha Karn.

"Warrow-hor junder mu!" the bandaged throg said proudly. Seeing Rathe's lack of comprehension, he frowned, then said in halting trade-talk, "We use dwarf-made thunder-barrel." He gestured widely with both arms. "Badoom!"

Rathe stood, astonished. Then a slow smile spread across his face. He turned to Jhen.

"Orvig's alive!"

"Uasru ki Ormandarn!" he said. *I am Ormandarn,* Rathe mentally translated. "Follow! We take you to dwarf and new Shaman."

The throgs let Rathe and Kelandra grab weapons from the dead guards, then hurried them through the corridors. The battle was still raging. The throgs moved quickly but cautiously, warily scanning each intersection, then dashing down straight passages. They heard shouts and screams, and running footsteps, and once a distant explosion. Several times they stepped over bodies. Many of them wore copper helmets, but many did not.

They found Orvig in a wide chamber. He was standing at a table, staring at what looked like a map, surrounded by a half-dozen armed throgs. The dwarf looked tired, but unhurt.

Ormandarn marched up to him. "Warrow!" he said.

"Garz?" Orvig replied absently. Then he looked up. "Rathe!" he shouted, and hugged him. He looked at Kel, then hugged her too. Laughing, Kel returned the embrace. Orvig pulled back, shook the throg's hand.

"Thank you, Ormandarn! It went well?"

"Well!" the throg said. He gave a tusky grin. "I go now," said Ormandarn. "Kill more bug-lovers!"

"Orvig! What's happening?" said Rathe.

"Can't you guess?" Orvig said. "The revolution!" He laughed. "Turns out quite a few throgs didn't like Gotha Karn's leadership — or his high-and-mighty copper-head thugs. They want to go back to the old days, when throgs fought their battles without insects, and leaders had honor, and everyone was equal under the Shaman."

"Jevaka Raye's doing?" Rathe guessed.

"Top marks, my boy." Another distant explosion shook the walls. "And Jhen and I made them a few tricks, as well. We Stonemelters know a few things about chemistry." He grinned.

"How'd you get away, Orvig?" asked Kel.

"Those secret passages I mentioned? Jevaka Raye's a canny old bird. He knew them all — he built most of them. We used them to slip past Karn's guards. So while Karn busied himself tormenting you and Kelandra, Jevaka Raye was contacting his partisans. We struck two hours ago. It took time to fight our way down here."

"I'd been wondering," Rathe said. "Why did Gotha Karn and his son leave Raye alive? It seems foolish."

"Jhen told me," Orvig said. "Karn got most of his magick from the crystal skull. He has power, but not knowledge. He's been trying to force Jevaka Raye to tell him how things work. He thought that blinding the old man would make him harmless." Orvig laughed shortly. "About as harmless as a boot full of scorpions. Glad he's on our side."

"How's the fight going?" Rathe asked.

"Hard to say," said Orvig. "Gotha was taken by surprise — he hadn't thought Jevaka Raye would move so fast. Hadn't realized how hated he was. The rebels have the numbers — but Gotha's guard have better weapons, and the Whispering Death only obey him. He's barricaded in the upper part of the stronghold with about fifty of his followers. Old Jevaka and six-score throgs are outside, besieging him. Everyone else is lying low." Orvig sighed. "It'll be bloody. The siege could take days."

Ormandarn and another throg had just reentered the room, pushing a shuffling line of bound prisoners. Rathe recognized one of the faces: Parlock Karn, the Shaman's son. A plan crystallized.

"Days? Maybe not," Rathe said. "I think I have an idea."

They stood halfway up the volcano throgs called eh-Doric-al-Kar, "The Eye That Had Once Burned." Last night Gotha Karn's son had led them to it, spurred by Kel's hissing threats and his own desire to ingratiate himself with Jevaka Raye. Rathe had been right... the man who had thrust his own guard onto an enemy sword had been happy to betray his father to save his own life.

Rathe had been daunted by the prospect of scaling the volcano, but Parlock, desperate to win favor, had shown him a narrow stone path, cunningly hidden, that wound its way up the mountain's rocky slopes. The climb had been easy. The path had taken them to the stone door, the entrance to the temple.

"This is the place your father spoke of?" Rathe asked.

"Kyas," said Parlock, with a poor imitation of enthusiasm.

Now it was dawn. The morning sun had just appeared over the volcano's peak, warm and bright. It was the first sunrise Rathe or Kelandra had seen in two days. With Orvig, they had traveled hard through the night. Now the three friends enjoyed a moment's rest, their goal in sight, savoring the feel of sun and wind on their bare arms.

The throg kneeling at their feet obviously didn't appreciate it. He covered his eyes and moaned softly.

"Get up, Parlock Karn," Rathe told him. "It's only the sun."

The sunlight illuminated a great archway, cut into the living rock of the mountainside. Columns stood on either side. One had fallen into ruin. The other depicted a many-branched tree.

"Let's go inside," Rathe said. He glanced back at Orvig and Kel. "It's odd," he told them. "I feel like I'm coming home."

Rathe walked through a huge echoing space, as dark as a womb. At first he thought he drifted, but then Orvig lit a lamp, and they were in a columned hall, and Rathe realized the slippery floor was solid under him, thick black glass. Around them was darkness, as though they stood on a pedestal within the cave. Ahead were fallen columns, scattered debris, piles of rubble that might once have been statues. Rathe caught glimpses of delicate faces, of animal limbs, of fragments of shapes he could not imagine, and ached to know what the statues had been, what they had meant. So much was lost . . .

Underfoot crunched shards of broken glass from the lamps that Rathe knew had fallen, long ago. But the temple, though damaged, was not destroyed. A pattern was etched in the glass floor — delicate carved lines that caught the light of Orvig's lamp, gleaming. With a start, he realized that he was following it, and he laughed, for he had done this once before.

"The rune forms a word," Rathe told the others. "A name. Thera's true name. He glanced back at the entrance. "I came through this arch before," he said wonderingly. "Only I was fleeing the temple, not entering it. It's like I'm walking through a dream."

"You are," replied Kel. "Thera's dream." She gestured ahead, where the floor was cracked, and shards of glass lay scattered. "See where the rune is broken?"

"We'll fix it," promised Rathe. "If Jevaka Raye wins, he'll help us."

"Aye," said Orvig. "We have your ring for the template. We'll bring in artisans, and make her whole, if we can. But not yet. Let's carry on with your plan, boy. We have a war to win." He looked pensive. "I'm worried about Jhen."

The dwarf-girl had stayed with Jevaka Raye, helping the old Shaman prepare for the offensive they planned for the morrow.

Rathe turned to Parlock, who stood trembling beside him. "Show us where the skull was," he ordered.

The statue lay toppled near the altar. Not shattered, like the others, just headless: a skeleton, every tiny bone in perfect detail, carved from the black glass formed in the volcano's heart. Once it had stood man-high, a last guardian, an image of Death serving the temple of Life. But some power had overcome it, left its head severed for a greedy magicker to find.

"My father didn't break it," Parlock said, echoing Rathe's thoughts. "He found the skull on the ground beside it. He sensed its power — it was still alive!"

"But who did it?" Kelandra asked. "Someone must have broken the statue. Defeated it. But why did they just leave the head?"

"I don't know," Rathe said. "Perhaps..." He stepped forward and touched the statue. It was cool, smooth. He concentrated, focusing on his ring, on the rune, willing himself to pierce the veil of time. He felt himself sinking.

"Wake up, boy!" said Orvig. He shook him. "Wake up!"

Rathe realized he had fallen to his knees. He looked up, met his friends' worried eyes. "I'm all right," Rathe said. He brushed sweat from his brow. "I saw it."

"What did you see?" said Orvig.

Rathe was still shaking his head. "It was veiled, shadowed. But I saw a little." He glanced at Kelandra. "You sensed it, when you cast the runes day before. You warned us. A third force. Hidden by illusions, veiled in lies, mad, greedy, amused by death...

"I remember," said Orvig. He shuddered. "What was it?"

"I don't know, exactly," said Rathe. "Sometimes it seemed huge, battling the crystal statue. Then small, like an evil goblin, hiding in the dark, hiding the skull so Gotha Karn would find it, and become his pawn." Rathe shook his head. "I don't know what it was, what it wanted. Maybe just mischief..."

"Whatever it wanted," said Kel, "it's gone now." She looked at the statue.

"Orvig, Kel — help me lift it."

Together they heaved the headless skeleton to its feet. Rathe half expected the glass bones to rattle and move, but the statue was solid and heavy.

"What do you plan?" said Kelandra.

Rathe raised his ring, so it caught the light of Orvig's lamp. He remembered the spell he had, unknowingly, performed in the dungeon to call back his stolen ring.

"A simple spell," said Rathe. "For we are simply restoring what has been. A spell of calling. And of renewal." He stepped behind the statue. "Hold my hand," he told Kelandra, "and think of Thera's rune." He touched the statue. "And imagine it whole. Look at the statue, and imagine it as it should be."

In the dark depths of Carkulroth, dawn had brought no end to battle. Perhaps Gotha Karn had sensed something far away — or maybe he sought revenge for the capture of his son. Whatever the reason, in a burst of mad fury he had sallied forth, throwing all his remaining Tse'Mara and copper-helmed guards against the rebel forces in an all-out frenzy.

Taken by surprise, Jevaka Raye's warriors fell before the wave of chitin and steel. Then their barricades were down, and they were fighting for their lives. Now the battle raged through the great hall. The fighting was too close to use the thunder-barrels. Many rebels had broken and ran. Others had died fighting. Ormandarn and a handful of warriors remained before their blind chief, weapons ready, waiting to die in Jevaka Raye's defense. With them stood a small dwarf girl, eyes determined, holding a sword with both hands.

Secure behind a wall of guards, Gotha Karn laughed, exultant. *Jevaka Raye was doomed! He was still the true Shaman!* A dozen fresh Tse'Mara hovered above him, wings buzzing. He held his skull aloft, and pointed to the small knot of defenders, willing the insect-creatures to rend and tear and slay. He began to give the order —

And the skull turned in his hands, its eyes burning into his. A soundless cry of exultation shook the room. Then Gotha Karn's hands were empty.

Thunderstruck, the shaman stood there. Gone! His power was gone! He felt his control go, magickal webs fading like shadows in the hated sun.

"Wahooka!" he screamed, half a prayer, half a curse. "You swore!"

Then he felt psychic leashes snapping, the breaking of magickal chains that bound a dozen savage wills.

The Tse'Mara struck at the thing that had bound their souls.

The last thing Gotha Karn heard was the whisper of death.

Epilogue

Kelandra stretched sinuously on the sleeping furs, then turned to face her lover. She lit a lamp, and studied his face. Rathe seemed older — yet younger too. The lines of care and worry had vanished.

Rathe's eyes opened. "I love you, Kel," he said.

"Tomorrow we marry," she replied. She stroked his hair. "In the temple."

"Tomorrow," Rathe said. He leaned over and kissed her for a long time. She broke away, laughing. "We have a lot to do today, you know! Orvig will be knocking soon!"

"He's worked wonders with his new assistant," Rathe said. Reluctantly, he released Kelandra. "That throg girl, Rhyanis. He says she could be a Master someday. There's a wonder for you — a throg craftmaster of Stonekeep. And thanks to the Stonemelter arts, the rune is repaired. Orvig doesn't want to seal that temple... he'd rather everyone come admire his work. His and Rhyanis' work, that is."

"Hmm," said Kel. "I never thought I'd be grateful to throgs." She moved gently against him. "And I would share but one rune with you." She traced a symbol on his forehead. "Aphros. The rune of love."

"But Thera will be good to us," Rathe said. "I can feel it. I had a dream, this night," he said. "A voice came to me. It was Thera." Rathe paused. "I thought we had won a great war, freed her from Khull-Khuum. But..."

"I know," said Kel. "I heard her too." She closed her eyes, recalling Thera's words.

This was just one battle, my children. I am still bound. At most, you loosened a finger just a bit. But I am a goddess. With one finger, and enough time, I can do a great deal...

How much time? Not in your children's day, or your grandchildren's. But I think... perhaps one of your grandchildren's children can take the final step with me.

You have my blessing, for what it's worth... and my promise that your line will endure, to fight for me again.

And it was so...